The Eridanos Library 5

Michel Leiris

Nights as Day,
Days as Night

Translated by Richard Sieburth with
a foreword by Maurice Blanchot and
an introduction by Roger Shattuck

Eridanos Press

Contents

Introduction

by Roger Shattuck and Roland Simon

Michel Leiris is our Montaigne. Instead of serving as mayor of Bordeaux, Leiris has served as director of the Musée de l'Homme in Paris; it houses one of the best and earliest collections of ethnography and primitive art. Instead of hobnobbing with kings and nobles, he has worked closely with major artists and intellectual figures of our time—Picasso, Jean-Paul Sartre, André Masson, Aimé Césaire, Roger Caillois, Georges Bataille. After the age of thirty, he channeled the greater part of his literary energies into a sustained autobiographical enterprise that began with *Manhood* (*L'Age d'homme,* 1939) and continued in the four successive volumes of *Rules of the Game* (*La Règle du jeu,* 1955–76). In all his works Leiris writes with a passionate detachment and digressive freedom that find their clearest precedent in the frankness of Montaigne's *Essays.*

Leiris started his exploration of dreams even earlier than his autobiography. Barely in his twenties, while associated with the older poet Max Jacob, Leiris began recording his nocturnal life and continued to do so. In

ix

1925 and 1926 Pierre Naville and André Breton published several of these fragments in early numbers of the review, *La Révolution surréaliste*. After a small edition in 1945, Leiris collected many of these dream narratives in 1961 under the title *Nuits sans nuit et quelques jours sans jour*. This is the volume Richard Sieburth has translated here with care and affection.

One expects little continuity in such a collection covering thirty-five years. What these free-standing pieces gradually create is a profound sense of interference intimately related to the visionary universe of the great French romantic poet, Gérard de Nerval. The first sentence of *Aurélia*, Nerval's final account of his tragic struggle with second sight and insanity, provides Leiris's epigraph. "Dream is a second life." Five pages later Nerval opens his narrative. "Here begins what I shall refer to as the encroachment of dream into real life." In Leiris's book that encroachment or interference takes the form of eleven sequences labeled "lived" (*vécu*) and a smaller number labeled "half sleep" interspersed with genuine dreams. Such a juxtaposition signifies that in certain waking experiences Leiris discovers the deeply etched, eerie vividness of dream. For example: the glimpse from a tramway of an oddly clad man carrying a long pole bedecked with automobile horn, open umbrella, and flowers; the sensation of groping back toward the hole in time caused by being anesthetized for an operation. Leiris refers obliquely to this overlap of dream and reality in the note printed on the back cover of the French edition.

> Dream is not an escape. Our night thoughts—even the most bizarre—come out of the same crucible as our day thoughts. We cannot expect to shake off

in sleep the desires, fears, or mere turn of mind that shape every phase of our existence.

Dream is not a revelation. If a dream affords the dreamer some light on himself, it is not the person with closed eyes who makes the discovery but the person with open eyes, lucid enough to fit thoughts together.

Dream—a scintillating mirage surrounded by shadows—is essentially *poetry*.

Considering this peremptory statement, it is surprising that Leiris omitted from *Nuits sans nuit* his earliest published dream, one of the most poetic. (He included it instead as a prose poem in *Haut Mal.*)

My body is traversed by a cluster of invisible lines which link each point of intersection to the center of the sun. I move about unharmed among all these threads which pierce me, and every point in space breathes a new soul into me. (*La Rèvolution surréaliste*, no. 2, January 1925)

This could be the voice of Nerval, or even of Swedenborg, testifying to his sensible connection with every part of the universe.

To grasp the flickering allusions and spiritual range of *Nuits sans nuit*, one needs a rough notion of how Leiris has moved within the intellectual and aesthetic currents of our era. Born in 1901 and thus too young to participate in World War I, Leiris began study in chemistry and soon turned toward literature. His earliest volume of poems, *Simulacre* (1925), is dedicated to the painter André Masson, who introduced Leiris to the group of writers and artists soon to launch Surrealism. Leiris's collaboration with the group arose primarily from his devotion to dream narratives, a favored surrealist genre practiced as an alternative to the rejected conventions of poetry and the novel. He also developed word play and punning into a sustained method of disinterring unsuspected significance from language. Leiris's successive "Glossaries" of semi-imaginary meanings based on expanded sound associations represent one of the major monuments of Surrealism. He prefers to probe succulent words like *féconder, luxure, mauve, torse*. During the mid-twenties Leiris married Louise Kahnweiler, who would later open the successful Galerie Louise Leiris in Paris, and made his first contact with Africa on a trip to Egypt with Georges Limbour. Leiris's father's death introduced a note of anguish lined with irony that affects the tone of his later writing.

The break with the surrealists for personal and political reasons came in 1929. While continuing to write poetry, Leiris contributed to Bataille's short-lived review, *Documents*, a number of critical essays on moral and aesthetic questions. In 1931 he joined the first major ethnological expedition through Africa (Dakar-Djibouti) directed by Marcel Griaule, disciple of Marcel Mauss, the founder of ethnology. Mauss's work on the social functions of the sacred had a decisive influence on Leiris. He soon chose ethnology as his profession and edited his African journals into the remarkable study *L'Afrique fantôme* (1934). When he joined Bataille and Caillois in 1937 to found the independent College of Sociology, Leiris gave a talk on "The Sacred in Daily Life." Mauss's ethnology had not carried him too great a distance from Surrealism.

After a year's military service in Algeria in 1939, Leiris spent most of the war in Paris writing his autobiography and occasionally sheltering fugitives sought by the Nazis. After the war his work with Sartre editing *Les Temps modernes* drew him toward Marxist political activity directed primarily against colonialism. His ethnological studies, growing out of trips to China, Africa, Haiti, and Cuba appeared in parallel with the publication of the four volumes of *La Règle du jeu*. Politics, poetry, ethnology, and autobiography do not represent conflicting activities for Leiris, whose writing has never been undertaken in the service of any one cause. His ambitious goal to "square the circle" of life, of his own life, declares itself in these different genres. One of his last collections of prose pieces, *Le Ruban au cou d'Olympia* (1981), contains a ferociously humorous attack on the pretensions of modern criticism. He gave the piece the untranslatable title, "Modernité/merdonité." Language itself, with its sudden revelations and secret recesses, proved to be an inspiration as inexhaustible as the turnings of his own mind.

Nuits sans nuit does not display Leiris's dazzling feats of word play. But the apparent soberness of these dream fragments should not hide their irony. Themes of travel and death, swift passage among different moral and intellectual realms, variations on the ritual gestures of ordinary life—these elements circulate in a medium composed of wonder and muted laughter. An American poet informs us that in dreams begin responsibilities. Leiris suggests less insistently that in dreams we can smile across at life and catch sight of its pervasive poetry.

Translator's Note

Nuits sans nuit et quelques jours sans jour pursues an extended pun on the porous demarcation between waking and dreaming. A literal translation of its title would read: Nights without night and several days without day. Or, at a further remove: Nights without darkness and several days without light. My English title, *Nights as Days, Days as Night,* extends the play to *la nuit américaine*—"day for night." Cf. Nerval's last words, a (suicide?) note left on his aunt's kitchen table: *"Ne m'attends pas ce soir, car la nuit sera noire et blanche."* Don't wait up for me tonight, for the night will be black and white.

Though they are inextricable from his ongoing ventures as an autobiographer and ethnographer (dreams are the fieldwork of the self), Leiris has preferred to classify these *Nights* among his poetry. They are therefore best approached as prose poems, their skewed rhythms observing the cadences of dream—a Chaplin, say, dancing asleep on his feet.

A number of these translations first appeared in

Sulfur 15, edited by James Clifford, the most complete anthology of Leiris in English to date.

Maurice Blanchot's piece, "Rêver, Ecrire," written on the occasion of the publication of *Nuits sans nuits* in 1961, is here translated from his collection of essays, *L'Amitié* (Gallimard, 1971).

Dreaming, Writing

by Maurice Blanchot

I remember the spare, slender collection of books entitled "l'Age d'or" in which, alongside other French and foreign works (including volumes by Georges Bataille, René Char, Maast, Limbour, Leonora Carrington, as well as Grabbe and Brentano), the initial *Nights* of Michel Leiris appeared. Now that these dreams, companions of forty years, have been published in their chronological sequence and precisely as they were transcribed, we are tempted to read them as an addition to his life, or better yet, as a supplement to that project of self-description and self-understanding through writing which Michel Leiris continues to pursue without respite. This was perhaps the way I read them at the very outset, and I remember a striking dream that seemed to bring to bear on the night the same surveillance, the same investigation that the author of *L'Age d'Homme [Manhood]* has placed at the very center of his writerly concerns: *"Waking up (with a shriek that Z . . . muffles) from the following dream: as if to catch a glimpse of something, I insert my head into an opening that resembles an oeil-de-boeuf*

window overlooking a dark, enclosed area akin to those
cylindrical pisé granary silos that I saw in Africa. . . .
My anxiety derives from the fact that as I lean over this
enclosed area and get a glimpse of its inner darkness, I
am actually gazing into myself." [July 12–13, 1940].

One observes that the dreamer here in no way pursues
the project of introspection to which he seems so
attached during the day. At issue here is a translation
or a transcription of this project into the language of
the night, not its implementation; and the anxiety is
not provoked by the discovery of the disquieting
realities that might be gathered in one's innermost
depths, but rather by the motion of looking into oneself
and seeing nothing but the contraction of a closed,
unlit space. Three years later [March 19–20, 1943],
another dream comes back to this motion, now taking
itself directly as a theme: it is the dream of a dream that
is ending, but instead of rising toward awakening,
instead of struggling to emerge out of itself, the dream
surreptitiously invites the dreamer to find a lower exit,
that is, to plunge into the depths of another sleep that
will no doubt never end. What these two dreams have
in common, what is grasped and lived as image by
both, is the very motion of turning back: in the former,
it involves a turning back upon oneself, such as simple
imagery might ascribe to introspection; in the latter, the
dream turns back on itself as if to surprise or survey
itself, thus identifying itself with an inverse vigilance,
a second-degree state of wakefulness in search of its own
limits.

This turning-away motion is characteristic. The
person who dreams turns away from the person who
sleeps; the dreamer is not the sleeper: at times dreaming
that he is not dreaming and therefore that he is not
sleeping; at times dreaming that he is dreaming and

hence, by this flight into a more inner dream, convincing himself that the first dream is not a dream, or else knowing that he is dreaming and then waking up in an identical dream which is nothing else but an ongoing escape from dream, which is an endless plunge into a similar dream (and so on and so forth through various twists and turns). This perversion (whose troubling implications for the state of waking Roger Caillois has described in his invaluable *L'incertitude qui vient des rêves*), seems to me related to a question that crops up naively and treacherously each and every night: Who dreams in dreams? Who is the "I" of dreams? Who is the person to whom this "I" is attributed, admitting that there is one? Between the person who is sleeping and the person who is the subject of dream events there is a fissure, a hint of an interval, a difference in structure; clearly it's not someone else, an entirely different person, but what exactly is it? And if, upon waking, we hastily and greedily take possession of the night's adventures as if they belonged to us, do we not do so with a certain sense of usurpation (as well as gratitude), do we not carry with us the memory of an irreducible distance, a peculiar sort of distance, a distance between self and self, but also a distance between all the characters and the various identities (however certain) we confer on them, a distance without distance, illuminating and fascinating, somewhat like nearing the far-off or making contact with remoteness? Such events and questions refer us back to an experience often described of late—the experience of the writer who writes the word "I" in a narrative, poetic or dramatic work without knowing who is saying it nor what relation this "I" bears to himself.

In this sense dream is perhaps already close to

literature, at least to its enigmas, its tricks of magic, and its illusions.

But let me return to Michel Leiris. For a man so deeply concerned with himself and so intent on explaining himself, the reserve he maintains vis-a-vis his dreams strikes me as remarkable. He notes them or, more precisely, he writes them. He does not ask questions of them. This is not mere cautiousness; it is well known that there is nobody more intrepid than he when it comes to inspecting the self, a process in which he invites us to participate by his own reckless frankness. He is knowledgeable, moreover, about psychoanalysis; he knows its mythology, its ruses, its boundless curiosity; more than anybody else, he would certainly be able to undo his dreams and read them as documents. Which is precisely what he forbids himself to do, and if he publishes his dreams it is not so that we might enjoy the pleasure of deciphering them, but rather so that we might display the same discretion, taking them for what they are, accepting them in their own light, and learning to seize in them the traces of an affirmation that is literary rather than psychoanalytical or autobiographical: These were once dreams; they are now signs of poetry.

Naturally we must admit that an exactness of relation obtains between the dream state and the writing state. It's not a question of making a literary work out of nighttime elements that have been transformed, embellished, perverted, or mimed by poetic means. Precision is part of the rules of the game. Writing takes hold of dream from the outside; the presentness of dream coincides with the non-presence of writing. At least this is the postulate of the enterprise that might be formulated as follows: I dream, therefore it gets written. [*Je rêve, donc cela s'écrit.*]

Let us in turn dream about this supposed kinship of dreaming and writing, not to mention speaking. The person who wakes up in the morning experiences a curious urge to *tell:* he immediately seeks out some listener whom he would like to have participate in the wonders he has just undergone, and is occasionally somewhat surprised to discover that this listener does not share in his amazement. There are dark exceptions—fatal dreams—but for the most we are happy with our dreams, we are proud of them, filled with the naive pride that might befit authors, convinced as we are that we have created an original work while dreaming, even though we refuse any responsibility for it. One should nonetheless ask oneself whether such a work truly seeks to become public, whether every dream seeks to speak itself, even though it be in a veiled manner. The ancient Sumerians were convinced that dreams should be recounted, recited. This was so that their magic power could be released as quickly as possible. Recounting the dream was the best way of avoiding its negative consequences; or one might decide to inscribe its characteristic signs on a slab of clay which one then threw into the water: the clay slab prefigured the book; the water, its audience. The wisdom of Islam nonetheless seems more sensible: the dreamer is advised to choose his confidant with great care or even to keep his secret to himself rather than revealing it to the wrong person. "The dream," it is said, "belongs to the first interpreter; you should only recount it in secret, just as it was given to you in secret. . . . And bad dreams should be recounted to no one."

We recount our dreams for some obscure reason: in order to render them more real, to share with someone else the singularity that belongs to them and that would appear to destine them to one person alone. But there are further reasons as well: to appropriate them and to establish ourselves, through our common speech, not only as the master of our dreams but as their principal actor, thereby decisively taking possession of this similar though eccentric being who was us over the course of the night.

Where does it come from, this eccentricity that marks the simplest of dreams and makes of them a present, a unique presence that we would like others to witness as well? The answer is perhaps already contained in the word itself. Lacking a center or rather slightly exterior to the center around which it is organized (or around which we reorganize it) and therefore situated at an inappreciable or imperceptible distance from us, lies that deep dream from which we can nonetheless not claim we are absent since on the contrary it brings with it an overpowering certainty of presence. But to whom does it bring it? It is like some presence that might well dismiss or else forget our capacity to be present in it. Do we not frequently get the impression that we are taking part in a spectacle not meant for us or that we are looking over someone's shoulder at some unexpected truth, some image we have yet to grasp? The fact is that we are not really there to grasp it: the show is being put on for someone who is not watching it in person and who does not have the status of a subject who is present. If dreams seem so foreign, it is because we find ourselves in the situation of strangers; and we are strangers precisely because the dreamer's self lacks any sense of true self. One could almost say that there is nobody in the dream and therefore, in a certain fashion, that there is nobody to dream it; hence the suspicion that when we are dreaming there is also someone else dreaming, someone who is dreaming us and who in turn is being dreamed by someone else, a premonition of that dream without a dreamer that would be the dream of the night itself. (An idea that from Plato to Nietzsche, from Lao Tse to Borges, recurs at the four cardinal points of dream thinking.)

Yet in this space that is as it were suffused with an impersonal light whose source escapes us (we almost never manage, even after the fact, to determine the lighting of dreams: as if they retained their clarity—diffuse, lambent, latent—in the absence of any precise center of light or of vision), there are nonetheless figures whom we manage to identify, among whom the very figure who figures us. In Michel Leiris's *Nights*, not only do we meet the author at various periods of his life but we also meet friends of his who have kept their own names and perhaps even their own faces and customary mannerisms. To be expected. Resemblances abound in dreams, for everyone in them tends to be extremely, wondrously similar: in fact, this is their only identity, they resemble, they belong to a domain that scintillates with pure resemblance: a resemblance that is sometimes steady and fixed, sometimes unstable and adrift (though always certain), fascinating and stirring each and every time. Consider the powerful spell a chance passerby can cast on us if, for a split second, he bears a resemblance; we are drawn to his face; it haunts us; familiar and distant, it also frightens us a bit; we quickly try to identify it, that is, to erase it by guiding it back into that circle of things where actual human beings are so bound up with themselves that they are without resemblance. A being who suddenly starts "resembling" takes on a distance from real life, passes over into another world, enters into the inaccessible proximity of the image while nonetheless remaining present, though his presence is not his own or somebody else's—an apparition who transforms all other presences into appearances. And this resemblance, during the (infinite) space of time that it asserts itself, is not merely some vague relation to a specific individuality; it is resemblance pure and simple—neutral as it were. Whom does the resembler resemble? Neither this person nor that: he resembles no one, or an elusive Somebody—as is clear in the case of corpses, when the person who has just died begins to resemble himself, solemnly rejoining himself via his likeness, gradually fusing into this beautiful, foreign, impersonal being who is like a double slowly surfacing from the depths.

The same holds true for dreams: dreams are sites of similitude, mediums saturated with resemblances, in which some neutral power of similarity, existing prior to any particular designation, is constantly on the lookout for a figure whom, if need be, it might activate into a likeness. It is Faust's mirror, and what he sees in this mirror is neither the young girl nor the likeness of her face, but rather resemblance itself, the undefined power of similarity, the infinite scintillation of reflection. And let us note that dreams are often traversed by the premonition of this game of resemblances that is being played out in them; how often do we wake up asking ourselves: Who is this creature? And right away, at the very same moment, we manage to match him or her up to such and such a person or to someone else and so on down the line, until we reach that point where the resemblance stops flitting furtively from figure to figure and agrees to reincorporate itself into a definitive form, submitting to the waking self which alone has the power to interrupt the process.

I will not pursue these reflections any further. We do not willingly admit that the dreamer only relates to himself through resemblance, that he too is a figure of the Similar—the non-identical—and that, given this similitude, he readily becomes anybody and anything. Still, this self seen in image, this self which is but an image of the Self and which is incapable of withdrawing into itself and therefore of putting itself into doubt, this self whose certainty is so rigid is indeed a strange self, no more a subject than an object, but rather the shadow of itself, a flickering shadow that frees itself from us like some replica that is more true because it is at once more similar and less familiar. In the depth of dreams—admitting they have a depth, a depth that is all surface—lies an allusion to the possibility of anonymous being, so that to dream is to accept this invitation to exist almost anonymously, beside oneself, drawn outside of oneself, released on the enigmatic bail of semblance: a selfless self, unable to recognize itself as such since it cannot be its own subject. Who (even upon the invitation of the evil genius) would dare transfer to the dreamer the prerogative of the Cogito? Who would allow him to state with utter assurance: "I dream, therefore I am"? One might at most suggest that he say: "Where I dream, it is awake" ["Là où je rêve, cela veille"], a vigilance that takes dream by surprise and that indeed comprises, within a present devoid of duration, the waking state of a presence devoid of persons, a non-presence in which no being ever occurs, and whose grammatical form would be the "He" that designates neither one nor the other: this monumental "He" that Michel Leiris anxiously sees himself become as he looks at himself in the empty, unlit depths of his silo.

Dreams are a temptation for writing because writing may well also deal with this same neutral vigilance that the nighttime of sleep seeks to extinguish but that the nighttime of dream awakens and maintains, even as it perpetuates being by a semblance of existence. More specifically, although it borrows the neutrality and the uncertainty that belong to the night, although it imitates this power of imitation and resemblance that is without origin, writing not only refuses all the agencies of sleep, all the facilities of unconsciousness, all the bliss of torpidity, but turns toward dreams because the latter, in their refusal to slumber off in the midst of sleep, constitute a further vigilance at the gathering point of the night, a lucidity that is always present, moving, captive no doubt, but therefore captivating. Sleep grows sleepless in dreams, and it is tempting to believe that this insomnia links us back, whether by allusion or illusion, to those waking nights that the Ancients termed sacred, nights laden with and devoid of darkness, long sleepless nights that correspond to the unmastered motion of inspiration that continues to allure us each time we hear something earlier speaking to us without speaking, indefinite in utterance, seeming to say everything to us prior to anything being said, perhaps actually speaking to us, but only in a semblance of speech. "Were it not for these horrible sleepless nights," wrote Kafka, "I would never write." And René Char, in less anecdotal fashion: *"Poetry lives on perpetual sleeplessness."* This is indeed what it lives on, undergoing this nightless night as Michel Leiris has called it, this night that is doubly nocturnal given this absence and subtraction of itself from itself, this night from which we too are subtracted and concealed and thereby transformed into something that remains awake, something that even as we sleep allows us no sleep: suspended between being and non-being. As Hölderlin reminds us in such precise terms: *"In the state between being and non-being, the possible becomes everywhere real, the real becomes ideal, and this, in art's free imitation, is a dream at once terrifying and divine."*

xxviii

Nights as Day, Days as Night

Le rêve est une seconde vie.

Gérard de Nerval

Very Old Dream

In front of a crowd of gawking spectators—of whom I am one—a series of executions is being carried out, and this rivets my attention. Up until the moment when the executioner and his attendants direct themselves toward me because it is my turn now. Which comes as a complete and terrifying surprise.

March 15-16, 1923

I am dead. I see the sky awhirl with dust, like the cone of air in a movie theater cut by the projector's beam. Several luminous, milky white globes are aligned in the far reaches of the sky. A long metallic stem grows out of each globe and one of them pierces all the way through my chest without my feeling anything but a great sense of euphoria. I advance toward the globes of light, slowly sliding along the length of the stem, ascending its gentle incline. In each hand I grasp those nearest me among a chain of other men who are also climbing toward the sky, each following the rail that skewers him. The only noise to be heard is the faint squeal of steel through the flesh of our chests.

One of my immediate neighbors is Max Jacob (who, for the past year and a half or so, has been giving me poetry lessons in my waking life).

April 11-12, 1923

Sauntering down a broad avenue, I pass by a huge, dark building that turns out to be a psychiatric hospital. The patients are out on the sidewalk, each one encased up to the waist in a small, round—or, more precisely, polygonal—cage with bars just like those protective railings that are normally placed around a manhole when its cover has been removed. The lunatics are all screaming and gesticulating, but none of them seem to think of escaping, which would nevertheless be easy to do. I recognize a number of people among them, notably Georges Gabory, wearing a gray overcoat that strikes me as being made out of plaster. I say hello to him and congratulate him on his book of poems, *Airs de Paris*. He thanks me and, having made sure that no guard can see him, emerges from his cage and then accompanies me on a long peregrination, whose various episodes I forgot upon awaking, but which is probably nothing but the logical counterpart to the stroll that, in the dream itself, presupposed our meeting.

April 12-13,1923

One evening, upon entering my room, I see myself sitting on my bed. With a single punch, I annihilate the phantom who has stolen my appearance. At this point my mother appears at a door while her double, a perfect replica of the model, enters through a facing door. I scream very loudly, but my brother turns up unexpectedly, also accompanied by his double who orders me to be quiet, claiming I will frighten my mother.

November 20-21,1923

Racing across fields, in pursuit of my thoughts. The sun low on the horizon, and my feet in the furrows of the plowed earth. The bicycle so graceful, so light I hop on it for greater speed.

December 22-23,1923

I meet a woman in a movie theater, I speak to her, I caress her. Arm in arm, we go back to the little bungalow where she lives, on a street that is a row of brothels. She opens the bungalow door and leads me to her bedroom: a young girl's room. She makes it clear that she is mine for the taking, but just as I am about to possess her, I am seized by second thoughts: this woman is a prostitute and most likely diseased. I leap into the garden with a single bound and jump (exactly as a woman would jump on a chair at the sight of a rat or large spider) on top of one of the two stone pillars that frame the entrance gate. I perch on this pedestal like a stylite.

As I am getting ready to leap down to the street, I realize that I am in fact on the uppermost platform of the Eiffel Tower, so I hold back. For a moment, I consider climbing down the outside of the tower, gripping the iron cross-bars. But knowing I would suffer a fatal bout of vertigo, I give up the idea and resign myself to waiting for the arrival of the next elevator.

The platform is at once a ship's deck, an airplane, the top of a lighthouse. I have no idea when I'll make it down.

July 27-28,1924

(*real-life*)

Having returned from Mainz, where he had been working as a journalist, and about to leave again for his native Le Havre, Georges Limbour—author of *L'Enfant polaire* and of those *Soleils bas* decorated by André Masson's prodigiously acute and airy etchings—was sharing my room in mother's apartment for a few days.

Around two in the morning, I wake up and see Limbour sitting on the couch he'd been using as a bed, casting a bewildered gaze around the room. The couch seems to be completely enveloped in gauze, as if covered with mosquito netting. When I ask him what's the matter, Limbour replies that he thought someone had hung drapery around the couch so as to imprison him. At which point the illusion vanishes.

The word *rêve* (dream) has something cobwebby to it, as well as something akin to the gossamer veil that clogs the throats of persons suffering from the croup.

This is no doubt due to its sonority and to certain formal connections between the *v* and the circumflex accent that precedes it (this accent being nothing more than a smaller, inverted *v*); hence the idea of interlacing, of a finely woven veil. Dreams are spiderlike, given their instability on the one hand and their veil-like quality on the other. If dreams are like the croup, it is probably because they are linked to the notion of nocturnal disturbances (like those bouts of false croup from which I suffered during the night as a very small child).

August 22-23, 1924

In a forest—which, when I'm awake, will seem like some sort of Brocéliande to me—I am walking with a friend (with no definite identity: basically just "a friend"). At a bend in the path we see a comet pass by very slowly and so low to the ground that I am afraid its tail will set fire to the tree tops. The comet disappears. I hear a voice, extraordinarily tender yet rich, filtering through the branches and little by little filling the entire forest with its song. My friend announces that all the birds in the forest are dying. At this point the voice falls silent, signaling that no winged creature remains alive in the underbrush.

We reach the edge of a pool, at the bottom of which I imagine nixies or other fairy-tale creatures are sleeping. The comet returns, hovers over our heads for an instant, then drops behind the horizon with a long shriek. The water of the pool then grows more transparent and I see that it contains towers and palaces with crowds of humans and animals, whom I know to be imaginary and not substantial, filing down their steps. I recognize among these beings such fairy-tale heroes as Bear Skin, Donkey Skin, and Puss 'n Boots. Emerging from the water, they proceed to dance with each other and drag me into a round from which it seems I will never escape.

That morning, the fish settled in the nests of vanished birds. The initial sentence of a story about the Flood that my close friend Roland Tual claimed he was working on at the time. My ill-defined dream companion may well be this friend who never published anything but was a wizard at fabulous oral mythologies.

August 25-26, 1924

A street on the outskirts of town, at night, among vacant lots. To the right, a metallic pylon whose crossbeams blaze with huge electric lights. To the left, a constellation reproduces in reverse (base skyward, tip earthward) the exact shape of the pylon. The sky is covered with blossoms (dark blue against a lighter background) identical to the floral configurations of frost on a windowpane. The lights go out one by one, and as each is extinguished, one of the corresponding stars also disappears. Soon total darkness falls.

October 13-14, 1924

With a group of tourists who, like us, have just landed in some provincial town, Georges Limbour and I are exploring a hotel we know to be a house of ill repute. As we follow behind the maid who is acting as our guide, we look this way and that through half-open doors with the hope of discovering something arousing. But we come across nothing. Tired of waiting, Limbour finally makes his way to the toilets, thinking that might be the place to find some adventure.

I continue along my way, but an old woman suddenly calls me over. I follow her. She leads me through a wall whose base she lifts up like a lid. I have to squat down in order to crawl through. She follows me.

We are in a vast room without any sort of decoration. Instead of a bed, an immense stone bathtub, a swimming pool of sorts, in a small adjoining room, slightly lower and serving as an alcove. It is very bright; moreover, the room opens directly (no window, simply a missing wall) onto the sunny countryside. I notice that we are more or less at the level of a second or third story. A large muddy stream, flows by the edge of the room. A tramp is sleeping on the bank of this stream, his knees tucked up and his head in his hands. A poodle sits nearby.

The old madam went to summon one of her girls and now I am patiently waiting with her. She fills me in about the girl, mentioning that one of her steady clients is a horribly ugly old man whom I know by sight. While the old woman is talking I get up to take a look outside and notice the dog using its head to butt its master into the river: the tramp topples over and, without so much as changing his posture, rolls to the edge of the stream and disappears into the water. The ripples created by his plunge soon dissipate. I am convinced he has drowned. But suddenly a hand emerges and I see the tramp reappear, swimming for his life even though he is still sound asleep.

At this point the girl shows up. She is wearing the classic attire of her profession: a short, flimsy dress, a frilly slip or some other promising item of clothing obviously easy to remove. She is all smiles as she comes toward me. I take her hands and look at her without a word, simply signaling my approval. She seems gentle and docile. I am aroused and pleasantly surprised, given the fact that neither she nor I had any part in choosing each other. The madam withdraws and I exchange a few rather innocent caresses with the prostitute.

October 31-November 1, 1924

I am told the following anecdote in which Max Jacob plays the leading role:

Max drops in on a lady, renowned for her beauty, who receives him in her dressing gown and crosses her legs as she sits down without realizing her gown has slipped aside, revealing her thighs. Max, aroused, cannot take his eyes off her lap. She finally catches on, smiles ironically, rearranges her gown with a little pat of her hand, and says to Max:

—What are you staring at, Monsieur Max?

—The celluloid of your legs.

—What a fool you are: they're made of broken glass!

The entire piquancy of this anecdote lies in the finesse of her repartee.

December 8-9, 1924

(*second sight?*)

Roland Tual (a real charmer, with a fine nose for a good read and above all a dazzling conversationalist) maintains in the course of one of our frequent literary discussions that Parny is a far greater poet than Baudelaire. I strongly object to this (even though I am in fact no fan of Baudelaire's—I prefer and shall continue to prefer Nerval).

When I wake up, my breakfast is brought to me as usual with my daily newspaper *Le Journal*, which the concierge has slipped under the apartment door with the rest of the mail. The newspaper carries a story whose hero, an elegant and cultivated man, displays on his bookshelves at home—among other tomes indicating his intelligence and taste—the *Elegies* of Parny (the name evoking lamé fabric and cotton prints from Jouy) right next to *Les Fleurs du Mal*. The authors of *Chansons madécasses* and *A une Malabaraise* are the only two writers mentioned in the story, just as they were the sole topic of the dream conversation.

December 10-11, 1924

A beautiful American woman, a writer or an artist, makes an appointment to meet me in a hotel—a huge, ultra-modern luxury hotel. I suspect she is affiliated with some secret society that is out to get me but I decide to go meet her nonetheless. I am shown into a sitting room that connects to a smaller room through two open doors. I wait for a while. The American woman arrives and invites me into the adjoining room. But as soon as we cross the threshold, two men suddenly appear and lock the doors behind me: I am a prisoner. The American woman laughs in my face. I notice a window, open it, and am all set to leap from the windowsill. It's raining buckets. Just at that moment the American woman whistles into the handle of a dog-whip: a groom in livery hurls himself at me, seizes me around the waist, slams me against a wall, and claps me into irons that tightly bind my arms, wrists, and ankles. He pushes the button of some hidden mechanism: the section of the floor that I am standing on begins to sink slowly. Anticipating ghastly tortures and realizing that I am dreaming, I want to wake up. Normally when I want to put an end to a dream that's turning nightmarish, I throw myself off a cliff or out a window. But, in this case, to what avail since I am bound hand and foot? After several atrocious moments of anxiety, the idea occurs to me that if I jerk my right leg, I will be able to hurt myself on the ankle-iron that is binding me. I give myself a swift kick, scream out in pain and wake up.

December 16-17, 1924

One night, drunk, on the Boulevard de Sebastopol, I pass an old wretch of a man and call out to him. He answers: "Leave me alone . . . I am the master of the heights of cinema." Then he continues on his way to Belleville.

The Same Night

So distinctly do I see the relationship between the rectilinear movement of a body and a picket fence perpendicular to the direction of this movement that I let out an ear-splitting scream.

The Same Night

I imagine the rotation of the earth through space, not in some abstract or schematic fashion, the axis of the poles and the equator made tangible, but rather as it really is. The rumpled face of the earth.

December 17-18, 1924

In his studio Giorgio de Chirico shows me an album containing reproductions of his paintings. Each of these reproductions is accompanied by a handwritten note indicating the theme of the work, providing either a succinct description of the painting in question or a statement of what the artist intended when undertaking it. Read in sequence, these texts turn out to be a series of brief poems.

Upon waking, only a fragment of one of these texts will stick in my mind: "... épeurés et apeurés" [frighted and affrighted]—which is not a mere phonetic nicety; rather, the nuance implied by the difference of the initial vowels puts into play a number of distant meanings.

One of the paintings is entitled "Jupiter's Finger Passing through the Partition." The canvas depicts an empty room, dark, with receding walls. From the right wall there emerges an enormous finger, an index finger (probably) or else a middle or ring finger. No clear distinction between this room that is painted more or less as a trompe-l'oeil and the room that I'm actually in.

In another dream (which I had years ago but am unable to date even approximately because I didn't note it down anywhere), I was looking at a cubist still life hanging in a museum or some other exhibition. Suddenly it seemed to me that my entire person was about to become part of the painting, as if my very being had been projected into it by my gaze, and I was seized with fright: if the world is really *that way*, a world without perspective, how go about inhabiting it?

Undated

I observe the following bit of dialogue between André Breton and Robert Desnos, or I read it as if it were a fragment of a play with stage directions:

A.B. (to Robert Desnos). The seismoteric tradition. . .

R.D. (turns into a stack of plates).

Undated

My friend André Masson and I are soaring through the air like gymnasiarchs. A voice calls up to us: "World-class acrobats, when are the two of you finally going to come down to earth?" At these words, we execute a flip over the horizon and drop into a concave hemisphere.

January 20-21, 1925

(half-asleep)

I see the word "bât" [packsaddle] written in capital letters while apparently hearing the strains of a violin. Then there follows, without my reading the letters this time: *"convolutions . . . prismatic gloom . . ."*

January 21-22, 1925

I set out on an excursion boat from a small river port where pirate and corsair ships of the 17th and 18th centuries are moored. Every type of vessel is represented; there is even a steamboat similar to the tugs one sees on the Seine. The flagship is huge and is made up of two hulls linked together by a single deck, an arrangement that allows smaller boats to sail through the flagship widthwise and to pass under the deck as though it were a fixed arch. The sails are capable of only one movement: they can be lowered or raised like drawbridges or like wings, according to that simple up-and-down movement to which the flight of birds used to be so schematically reduced in sketches made by designers of flying machines.

The excursion boat takes me to the ruins of the abbey of Jumièges. After a long walk through the halls and stairways, I come across my brother lying in bed. I ask him what he's doing there. He replies that he is the director of the "Abbey Clinic," then (the dream now extending into a half-awake revery) he explains to me the ritual of the "Tactile Exam" that is observed in the region at various prescribed dates: a number of girls, naked, their faces masked, are gathered into one of the monastery's crypts; a young man, chosen by lot, leaves a nearby village at midnight and makes his way into the crypt blindfolded; his task is to feel up the girls until he has recognized one of them by purely tactile means, and if this girl also manages to recognize him in turn, he makes love to her. There is a similar game called "Aural Exam," in which the method of identification involves the voice.

Undated

(half-asleep)

The working drawing of a shape I would roughly describe by comparing it to the profile of a Pharaonic *pschent*, reduced to the crown of Upper Egypt alone, truncated at the top and without any framing in the front. It is the "hennin of the void." No line defines the base of this headdress (so that the design remains open to that side), whereas the tip—or the crown—is indicated by stippled lines forming an obviously convex lens, which I can only identify (in my revery) as a glass object that is called a "lens" in optics and that can just as easily be concave as convex. The words "stem or finger" and "finger or stem" run like captions along the length of the two curved lines whose double bulge outlines the profile of the *pschent*. All of this against a "black background of night," expressly designated as such.

March 14-15, 1925

Sidled up to a woman named Nadia—to whom I am drawn by very tender feelings—I am at the edge of the sea, a shore on the order of Palm Beach, a Hollywood beach. Playfully, just to scare me and to ascertain how hard I would take her death, Nadia, an excellent swimmer, pretends she is drowning. In fact, she does drown, and her lifeless body is brought to me. I begin to weep until the wordplay "Nadia, drowned naiad" [*Nadia, naïade noyée*]—which comes to me just as I am waking—appears to be both an explanation and a consolation.

March 20-21, 1925

A Scotsman with puffed-out cheeks blows into a bagpipe shaped like a gigantic bloated man, in the manner of Picasso's "Baigneuse."

May 7-8, 1925

Travels, railways. Before leaving Paris—or passing through Paris—I arranged to meet my mother in, for example, one of the forward cars of such and such a train at the Amsterdam Station. In my dream, I seem to be remembering an earlier dream that appears to provide a precedent for my current situation: having forgotten my suitcase on a train and having figured out the location of my compartment, I wait for the next train, convinced I will find my suitcase in the corresponding compartment; which is exactly what happens.

Undated

Several of us are wandering all over the face of the
continent by car, bus, and train. Crimes are taking
place in isolated stations; the hotels we stay in are
occasionally attacked by bandits and the thing to do
is to pack a pistol. I am a juror in a hick town and
witness an execution (no doubt that of a chamber-
maid).

In a street of one of the working-class suburbs of
Paris, one of my surrealist friends—Marcel Noll—who
is traveling with me, shows me the thirty-meter
mattress he always carries with him on his travels.
Two couples can sleep on it end to end but they run
the risk of losing themselves in the long tunnel of
sheets. When he's on the road the mattress serves as a
suitcase; Noll rolls his baggage into it and secures the
roll with a strap.

Rimbaud (or Limbour?) is also along in the guise
of a sickly child who physically resembles those kids
they call "jail bait." He goes through several cycles of

37

death and resurrection, like all the other characters in the dream.

In one of the towns we visit, on a large public square featuring a plaster statue (a gentleman in a frock coat who reminds me of the ghost of Gérard de Nerval who supposedly appeared in my bedroom one night), there is a prison whose pediment is engraved with the following words: "City Court House" [*Palais du Greffe*] an inscription I prefer to read "City Graft House" [*Palais des Greffes*], seeing as how it would thereby gain in significance. Small groups of women, fairly pretty but clearly riffraff by their shabby style of dress, are heading toward the monument. I hear them talking to each other. They are hurrying back to the penal colony where they are doing time; if they are late, they will be flogged or receive some other cruel form of punishment. This was their day off; they went to visit their mistresses and whiled away their time caressing them. For these women are lesbians; men want nothing to do with them, given their wretched clothing and shameful condition.

Accompanied by Z . . . (who is my current fiancée in waking life), I enter the penal colony. The first thing we see is a sort of cloister the length of which is lined with numerous children under the watchful eyes of aristocratic-looking women, no doubt of Anglo-Saxon origin, who are the wives of the jailers or rather of the "colonists," as they are called. The children are dressed in British fashion and carry leather school satchels under their arms. These are the sons of the convicts; they are waiting for school to start.

Beyond the cloister lies the entrance to the Museum. It is a place that reminds one simultaneously of the Grévin Museum, the Carnavalet Museum, the amusement park at the Exposition of Decorative Arts, the

38

Aeronautics Show I visited as a child, and the Garden of Tortures imagined by Octave Mirbeau. We are aware that this museum is some sort of Museum of Horrors and we make our way into it, dreading its enchantments.

At first things are not so frightening. The place is fairly dark and we see some devices that more or less resemble those dynamometers one finds at county fairs or at establishments devoted to these kinds of games, except that these were almost exclusively composed of moving multicolored electric lightbulbs: figures of demons. Further on, we come across huge stands that are almost completely dark. In the shadows one can vaguely make out some enormous airplanes built in the shape of birds' heads. These birds' heads have open beaks: the cockpit is located at the very bottom of the throat, a strange nocturnal space lit up by no more than two or three lights that gleam like precious carbuncles. The dome of the skull, about as tall as a six-story building, is a cupola made of canvas which functions as a parachute (here they call it a "hot-air balloon").

We are still not that terrified (true, some of the exhibits that we had been told were fairly frightening are out of order), but a bit further on the spectacle becomes truly horrific. There are, as in the Grévin Museum, wax figures that seem to be alive, but also living figures that seem to be made out of wax. These are the convicts. They are being submitted to atrocious tortures. Everywhere I see racks, torture boots, gibbets, corpses splayed on wheels, pillories, stairways littered with dismembered limbs, and every conceivable type of torture device or other contraption reminiscent of Piranesi's *Prisons*. In the first hall, torturers wearing white smocks are engaged in human vivisection.

We leave the Museum and board a steamship in order to visit the rest of the penal colony. An instrument that resembles a water level is set up on the center of the deck, next to the compass. A long vertical tube connects it to the sea and it measures, far more effectively than a waterline would, just how the ship should normally stay afloat. If the level drops, this indicates the ship is taking on water or that a major storm is approaching.

We are in the midst of a crowd of men, women, children, and animals. The ship is already well out to sea when a dreadful panic sets in: the water level has gone crazy, which means we are about to sink. All the passengers leap overboard and despite their efforts to stay afloat, they all drown. My fiancée and I, however, have kept our wits about us and remain aboard the ship which, despite a serious leak and heavy seas, manages to return to shore, depositing us safe and sound on terra firma.

We are congratulated for our courage and are shown a humorous engraving by an unknown artist in the museum catalogue that depicts either this very accident or else a similar accident that had occurred some time before on a ship belonging to the same company. I see passengers trying to swim for safety, bits of wreckage, and, floating upside down among the waves, tripods that look like kangaroos. But I learn these are, in fact, horses that had plunged headlong into the sea and drowned. Only their tails and stiffened hindlegs emerge from the water, which is why I mistook them for tripods.

April, 1926

(half-asleep)

A meat tree, each of whose roots bears a beefsteak.
One night a year, Jesus Christ appears among these
roots to proclaim the Republic. Whereupon the roots
turn into an inverted Christmas tree, laden with lights
and hams, with Jesus Christ, the Virgin Mary, and the
Apostles in a halo at its center.

Undated

After a protracted series of adventures—escaping from nighttime assaults in the gardens of Ranelagh, a trip on an ocean liner where there are thieves masquerading as detectives—I find myself with Z . . . (now my wife) in a sordid furnished room and am making love with her while looking at the following picture painted by our friend Georges Bataille.

Rectangular, wider than it is tall, the painting is cut in half by the line of the horizon. Above, the sky; below, the sea. In the upper right-hand corner (where the story begins, though I can only faintly remember it), a winged horse describes a downward trajectory—at a small distance above this and as if borne along by the same movement, there is a piece of seaweed covered with blood. Visibly drawn or simply imagined, the seaweed first veers toward the left and then, having gone nearly as far as possible in that direction after circling around an immense steel pin that rises out of the sea like a stake, the seaweed moves to the right and guides the horse—still continuing its downward course—to sea level, roughly in the middle of the lower half of the painting, where there is a raft carrying a vertical hand whose index finger points skyward. This raft (drawn at an angle and shaped like a parallelogram) turns out to be the horse—transformed into a raft upon plunging into the sea—and as for the hand, it is merely an avatar of the bloody seaweed.

Undated

Climbing a rocky ridge. There is a passage to be traversed made up of vulture nests vertically arranged like the niches of a columbarium. Just as I am about to cross it, I see a vulture circling close overhead and then roosting on a hillock overlooking the nests. If I traverse the passage by scaling up the nests, the bird will attack me. So I turn around and go back.

Undated

(half-asleep)

Gunshots in the night: a gigantic ram's head appears. Its two horns are two poles exchanging magnetic discharges. A woman, supine, bound hand and foot, suspended in the void, slowly passes between these two magnetic branches. A small veiny drawing on her breast becomes a laceration, then lightning in a cloud, and the ram's head lets its fleece hang down like rain.

Undated

(half-asleep)

A tree with three branches (that are snakes) taps at my windowpane, dressed in a ready-to-wear suit and a broken detachable collar.

Somewhat later that night, a dog I imagine to be lying between my mattress and my bedspring turns into a long bronze reptile whose porcupine-like quills penetrate my body.

Undated

I walk along a beach and risk being engulfed by the waves. I am wearing a top hat crowned by a flame that seems to be a Pentecostal fire. And I have long hair.

Undated

(daytime fantasy)

Headfirst, my arms pinned to my body, I am hurtling through a metal tube lined with spiral grooves, like a shell spinning down the rifled bore of a cannon in the wake of an explosion of gunpowder. As I shoot along, the barrel files my forehead like a grindstone.

Undated

I am lying in bed exactly as I would in reality, except that my forehead is pressed against the white powdery wall of a large cylinder made of lime, a cistern of sorts, exactly my height, and which is nothing other than *myself*, actualized and exteriorized. I feel this other exterior forehead against my own, and thus I imagine my head is pressing against the very substance of my mind.

September, 1926?

They are performing a play in London falsely attributed to Alfred Jarry; the stage decor is straight out of music hall revues, and chorus girls are doing a ragtime song-and-dance.

The main character is a Greek—with whom, though I am merely a spectator, I identify now and then—and one of the other characters, also a Greek, is a wizard.

In one of the acts, the hero imagines that a regiment of French soldiers is parading by him. Because he does not salute the flag, an officer (who is quite real) leaves the ranks, revolver in hand. First he trains his weapon on the soldiers, then on the crowd, and finally on the Greek, who is none other than myself. He aims at his right eye and, after several moments of suspense, fires.

Everything vanishes. Then we return to Ancient Greece. Shortly thereafter, the Greek goes blind in one eye (as if the gunshot he had received were merely the prefiguration of this infirmity); soon he goes totally blind, having fallen under an evil spell.

Undated

(*Le Havre*)

A postcard reaches me from someone called Timotheus Smollett (with whom, as the dream would have it, I had dealings during my real visit to Egypt where Georges Limbour was then teaching). The bottom of the card is marked "Le Havren"—which should be pronounced in German fashion and which serves as the photograph's caption. It depicts three pyramids of snow with very irregular ridges; although it appears to be an optical illusion, their summits actually blend into the clouds. Smollett writes me somewhat on the following order: "We are scaling these pyramids and often risking our necks." I understand this very well; after all, there are times when one has to walk on clouds.

Undated

I read or hear or articulate these words as though they constituted a title or a maxim whose meaning was self-evident and needed no additional elucidation:

L'oeil charnois

Hinge [*charnière*] of the furtive gaze [*regard en tapinois*], fleshy eye [*oeil charnu*], soft as camelskin [*peau de chamois*]?

Undated

My father has made himself an armband, insignia of his profession as a stockbroker. It is a sleeve of black luster toward the top of which he has embroidered in gold the image of a coat hanger whose shoulders are sloped like two parentheses.

He loads people into this armband in order to transport them to the Stock Exchange.

Undated

I meet a woman I supposedly knew some twenty years ago in London under shady circumstances. The woman, a friend of hers, and I are all booked on a flight—to London, as it turns out. But first I must go for a fitting at Macdougal's (a Parisian tailor who draws his inspiration from the land of *Lucia di Lammermoor* and whose establishment I have in fact patronized upon several occasions).

When my lady friend and her companion prepare to leave my place, I display an extreme reluctance to follow them. So extreme that I hear the man whisper to my lady friend: "So, doesn't he want to sleep with you?" But she reassures him, knowing as she does what's going on.

It is, in fact, not any lack of tenderness on my part that accounts for my reluctance, but rather the memory of a crime committed twenty years ago at Whitechapel by my friend, her companion, and myself. I had just been reminding her that this represented "the only bloodstain on my book of fate." And if this memory causes me to hesitate, it is because I *know* I will recognize the fitter who works at Macdougal's as our victim who miraculously escaped. Since those days when the fitter and I were both members of Jack the Ripper's gang (as I sketch out this horror-story episode, I forget that he worked alone, killing purely for his private pleasure), I have changed a great deal: I have become quite the dandy, whereas I used to be a slob. But I am afraid he will recognize me just as my lady friend did.

At long last, despite my fears (which I only mention in a very evasive fashion, even to her), I follow the two of them.

Undated

I am going on a trip, so I have to move all the books in my library from one room to another.

Since the occasion calls for me to show one of my manuscripts to some of my friends, I go down to the street, rip what appear to be streetcar tracks from the pavement, and go back up to the apartment, dragging meters of rails behind me that bang on the stairs with every step I take. I then realize that this load is in fact made up of a series of large glass objects similar to those coasters that used to be placed under the feet of the piano in middle-class living rooms to protect the carpet or the floor. Because this is indeed my manuscript, I am fairly annoyed. But I manage to console myself, given the fact that my arrival provokes the following comments: "He's quite something, that Leiris! You ask him for a manuscript, and he drags up rails from the street." On the other hand, though, these objects finally reveal themselves to be melting ice, and although the chain quickly dissolves, I hope I will be able to reconstitute some of its elements.

At the farewell dinner honoring my departure, I am seated beside my niece. My sister, who is also present, tells me that her daughter—this niece next to me—has just been "given her freedom in department stores," a legal phrase meaning that she now has the right to do her shopping all on her own. The employees of the store where the ceremony took place are all agronomists. They celebrated her emancipation because she is interested in agriculture, and they spoke to her of a revolution (the Commune?) which is an agrarian revolution in which she played a glorious agrarian part.

May 15-16, 1929

The setting is a theater where I am performing a play with a woman, both she and I truly feeling for each other the emotions we are pretending to act out. At the end of the performance, she drags me off to a place which (in retrospect) I would describe as a kind of stairwell squeezed into another stairwell. I take her in my arms to make love. Then I see her stretched out on the ground, naked.

Along the line that extends from her sex to her neck, passing through her bellybutton and the cleavage of her breasts, there is a growth of long, blonde weeds—damp, salty tufts planted at regular intervals. To me this woman then seems to resemble Z . . . or to be Z . . .

May 17-18, 1929

A chemist (whom as a matter of fact I knew when I was a chemistry student working at the Central Laboratory for the Prosecution of Tax Evaders) owns a luxurious estate where he is waited on hand and foot by "selectants"—automata, or young boys and girls reduced to robots.

In this dream, the rest of which is sheer confusion, a number of characters play a role: among whom, my mother, the wife of my friend Roland Tual, and the publisher who brought out my book that toed the surrealist line, *Le Point cardinal*.

May 29-30, 1929

Lined up single file, each one mounting the preceding one, eight dogs copulate before my very eyes. I am informed that they have been trained to do this as a stunt.

July, 1929

The scene takes place in a zoo that is also a menagerie. Before my very eyes, a lion leaps out of an ornamental pool and claws its trainer. The scene resembles a heraldic figure or, better yet, a symbolic image in a book of alchemy.

In the morning I learn that during the previous night a tiger had escaped from the Amar Circus, whose tent was at that point pitched not far from my house.

July 14-15, 1929

(half-asleep)

One of my incisors [*incisives*], having grown inordinately (as long and wide as a street), is cut vertically in half by a saw; the tooth thus becomes Venice [*Venise*].

Did this convergence of Venice and a sawed tooth come about via the word "laguna" which conjures up the idea of a lacuna? There is, moreover, the Rue de Venise which was for a long time the narrowest street in Paris.

July 18, 1929

(real-life)

A pole nearly as long as a fishing rod, with an automobile horn attached to it about a third of the way up and topped off by a very old, very dirty white umbrella which is in turn crowned by a bouquet of flowers. The umbrella is open and although it sits too high on the pole to cast any decent shade, the man who is strolling around with this contraption as if it were some archaic parasol seems to be using it both as a fashion accessory and as an actual protection against the sun. Could it be some sort of clever device that allows its bearer to produce rain or shine at will? Somewhere between forty and forty-five years old (and thus nearly an old man to my less than thirty-year-old eyes), he appears to be a working-class type—thin, a small moustache traced across his face, dressed all in black, with a filthy white sweater. He is wearing a black cap with a leather visor and around his neck there is a strand of large nickel-plated beads reminiscent of those women's necklaces that were in fashion a few years back.

I witness this on a sidewalk of the rue d'Auteuil—the street where I was born but where I have not lived since early childhood—looking out from a streetcar whose route was discontinued so long ago that I nearly ask myself if it ever existed in the first place.

August 29-30, 1929

I make the acquaintance of Liane de Pougy (such as she must have looked in her heyday) and am flirting with her.

September 3-4, 1929
(Sancerre)

There is an outdoor competition going on: a large group of women and girls, dressed in those ragged street urchin outfits you often see on American colored girls, but virtually bare-chested, have gathered in the forest underbrush, facing toward the sun. The winner of the contest will be the first woman whose nipples are simultaneously grazed by two sunbeams that have passed through the interstices of the branches and leaves.

September 6-7, 1929

It is the eve of the Russo-Chinese War and I am about to be sent off to battle as a simple foot soldier (we're still under the Czarist regime and, given our alliance, all Frenchmen of draft age are to be conscripted into the Russian army). Among other objects and under circumstances I cannot recall upon waking, I see a moderate-sized statue, fairly flat and oval in shape, representing a helmeted Minerva brandishing a single raised arm that she presses tightly against her head. It is her right arm and the entire figure (Minerva, helmet, topped by the straight line of the extended arm) possesses some profound significance that appears to reveal what war means to me but which, once the dream is over, I cannot precisely define.

Undated

"Leopold," the ever-so-charming departmental supervisor (moustache, gullible look, black jacket or morning coat) who disappeared—dead?—at the end of the dream. Wracked by grief, I shook the corpse or puppet by the shoulders and, my voice quivering with gentle emotion, repeated "Leopold! Leopold!" the way, as a child, I might have displayed my grief at seeing some ridiculous yet sophisticated toy lying there broken.

April 22-23, 1933

In a film, a female character—who is essentially a *mother*—briefly appears bare-breasted. At which point someone in the audience remarks: "She's good-looking, but her breasts are a little long . . ." I immediately gather that "long" is an ironically euphemistic term for "saggy."

Rereading this note, I remembered an expression that a schoolmate and I used to use in high school (at Janson-de-Sailly, somewhere between 1914 and 1916), but in a completely opposite sense. A section of the high school had been turned into a military infirmary, and among the Red Cross nurses we used to see around every day, there was one whose prominent, elegantly contoured bust we greatly admired. We dubbed her bust "ogival," proudly using an adjective which demonstrated our knowledge of medieval architecture, and enjoying ourselves like refined aesthetes whenever we uttered this sibylline term.

July 30-31, 1933

(*Kerrariot*)

After a few drinks at a bar, I expel a mixture of blood and vomit from my nose. I've come down with some sort of congestion.

Half-asleep, this incident strikes me as an image of death, more on account of the repugnant nature of the actual event than out of consideration for the unfortunate repercussions it might entail.

To have so vividly felt and imagined myself falling apart in this sordid manner is surely a sign that my nerves are shot! At least this is what I tell myself when I'm fully awake again, thus managing to shift my focus from the nausea induced by my distressing dream to another subject of anxiety. Although grounded in cool reasoning, is this any less nauseating for me who, for the past four years or so, has been making such a great effort to get back into the saddle?

70

August 19-20, 1933

(*Kerrariot*)

Discussing some film, allegedly an old silent in which the American comic Ben Turpin uses his celebrated squint to size up a nearby tree at a single glance—its trunk, its branches, its tip—and estimate its age by whether it's "shot up straight" or not. If the character played by Ben Turpin has such a remarkably wide field of vision, it is because he is so cockeyed that his two eyes cross at a very obtuse angle.

Is this the first segment of an extremely long dream made up of disparate elements, or the first in a series of dreams I had during a single night while on vacation in Brittany several months after returning from a long trip to black Africa? That night I met a great many people and visited an extraordinary variety of sites: a corner of Cairo or Barcelona; a gymnasium and a country fair located on two floors in the same building, one occupying a concert hall and the other a theater; the Place de l'Opéra where a broad stream

71

was flowing, probably in the wake of some political demonstration.

I long remembered the "corner of Cairo" and that beautiful tanned girl beneath the bluest of skies, making her way between the raspberry-colored houses whose *moucharabiehs* were windows describing half-arcs, decorated with small pilasters, with a demi-rosette set into the confluence of their curves.

August 22-23, 1933

(*Kerrariot*)

One of my friends, a colonist, lives with four women in a distant land.

One of these women is (probably) a young Maori. I see her on the beach in the company of a very pleasant older woman, as well as a number of other people. She is naked, and I notice the color of her skin: very white, almost uniform in hue, her lips and nipples virtually colorless. Of average height and somewhat fleshy in appearance, she has muscles that are very soft to the touch even though they are in fact firm and knotty. I caress her right arm and shoulder and proceed to stretch over her body. But thinking we are not alone, I content myself with sitting by her side, and we remain in that position, as if lolling on the sand after a swim.

The three other women are Japanese, very slender, the features of their faces sharply defined, not at all doll-like. Fake Japanese, no doubt. The colonist is carting them about in some sort of small paper wagon that serves as a trailer. I make my way into the wagon from the rear by lifting up a paper curtain. All three women are naked. Their retreat, their giggles, their shrieks of confusion. Then (I think) we have tea together. I chat with one of them (she is the only one whose face I remember upon waking, the face upon which I modeled my description of all three women, making no distinction between them). She informs me that the colonist makes love to the three of them alternately. This takes place in utter darkness so that at no point can they identify their partner or be sure there are not in fact several of them.

This entire episode, so fresh and so simple that one could scarcely characterize it as erotic, is merely the high point of a dream that features other elements relating to the journey I have just made through the tropics from Dakar to Djibouti: a stay in Abyssinia (though it might be in the mountains or in Canada); scientific or administrative tasks upon my return from the mission; reproaches from one of my sisters-in-law concerning my conduct toward my wife: I am wrong to leave her alone with one of my colleagues from the mission, to which I reply that I have complete confidence in her and that I would step in immediately were I to find out that my colleague had had the poor taste to try something. In this portion of the dream, I display (like most males) as much distaste for polyandry as I had felt a liking for polygyny in the central episode of the night.

August 25-26, 1933

(*Kerrariot*)

André Gide recounts a crime that is a symbolic parricide. The crime in question was committed recently (indeed, it was reported in the newspapers): a madman hacks to death a little boy and girl who were playing "bride and groom." In the dream the crime is a parricide because: 1) the hostility against children playing "bride and groom" is a manifestation of the Oedipus complex; 2) the murderer had already "ripped off a streetcar" and had crashed it into a station that was a substitute for his father; 3) going right for the midriff, he had also struck someone with a pickaxe.

September 3-4, 1933

(Kerrariot)

In the company of E. Tériade and very likely Albert Skira (then joint directors of the magazine *Minotaure* whose second issue was devoted to the ethnographic mission from which I had just returned), I am proceeding through the underground passageways of an immense rock formation. Tériade is acting as the guide and we visit some "churches beneath the crypts," gothic-style chapels crudely carved into the rock like rough alveoli (probably inspired by the rocky Breton coast with its jagged wayside crosses, as well as by the churches of Lalibala, ethnographic curiosities I am familiar with by reputation). One of these chapels contains a block of stone that has scarcely been hewn and is supposed to represent a chimera or some other monster of human dimensions, a sort of gargoyle not unlike the ones that used to be shown to me for my viewing pleasure on postcards or on sight-seeing trips.

Some time elapses and the chapel is no longer a crypt. No vault (even though today I am unable to positively maintain that there was an open sky over the place). But fairly high overhead, the interior of the edifice is encircled by some sort of balcony, the kind one sees around certain hotel lobbies or dance halls. In fact, the building is indeed a hotel: at the center of the nave that constitutes its lobby there is a harmonium at which a musician is sitting—a purely visual character to whom my memory will ascribe no sound whatsoever. All the rooms opening out onto the balcony are situated high enough over the lobby so that the noise of the mass will not disturb their guests. The harmonium is placed in such a fashion that it can also be used for jazz when the lobby is turned into a dance hall. My companions and I take a table near the dance floor and have coffee. A bit of coffee spills into my saucer and, despite the rules of etiquette, I pour it back into my cup, thus rescuing this precious liquid that I have always found too great a delicacy to waste.

Then I go see the sights of Paris like a tourist, visiting Notre-Dame in the company of someone I got along with very well during high school (a boy named after one of the four Evangelists and whose good behavior hid a rather sharp sense of humor). The cathedral is enormous and makes up a single building with the Sainte-Chapelle. A guide (a professional this time) leads the group of visitors through the stairways. My friend and I, more eager to play hooky than to listen to the guide, each sneak off on our own to see whatever it is he refuses to show us. In the course of my explorations, I happen across a stairway that leads up to a jube, which is in fact a long banquet table (a possible reminder of an event that took place the previous day: a banquet given at Trebeurden to inaugurate a monument to Aristide Briand). I have to pick my way among the place settings without disturbing their layout, taking care not to prick myself on the table decorations that seem to be made out of thorny branches. By a stairway that leads down from the middle of the table, I leave the jube—this jube that seems to have been set up for some jubilee—and I join my confederate down in the nave.

We then proceed to a public square which is the terminus of the 248 bus, the place where my wife and I had arranged to meet. But a map posted in the bus shelter shows that the terminus of the 248 is located on another square. Given this fact, I wonder how we will manage to join up. Should I wait here or go to the correct terminus?

I awake and have breakfast in the hotel room that we must leave the following day to return to Paris. As I am washing, I look at the breakfast tray that my wife has placed in front of the fireplace—as she usually does when we're finished. Next to the teapot and empty cups lie two branches of thistle she had tossed there while tidying up. I remember that the jube appeared to be a banquet table on which some thorny branches (probably) had been arranged. Shortly thereafter, I look at the tray again and notice a pack of Gillette razor blades I had forgotten I had tossed there after having given the last blade to my wife's brother. I connect the presence of these Gillettes (i.e., objects that can wound you) to my fear of the thorny branches in the dream.

As I write this all up, basing it on notes that are more than twenty-five years old, I am struck by a detail whose singularity stands out for me only today. The numerals 2, 4, 8 in the number of the bus are the first three integers in a geometric progression based on the number 2. And indeed, duality seems to be the connecting thread in this dream: the co-directors of the magazine *Minotaure;* the double function of the hall I'm in, at once church nave and hotel lobby; the twinning of Notre-Dame and the Sainte-Chapelle; the doubling of the bus terminus, representing a threat to the reconstitution of my wife and myself as a couple. Was it not a fact that the two or so years I had spent travelling had practically estranged us? Was it not true that from that point on my professional life would find itself between two stools, seeing as how my work as an ethnographer would now be superadded to my activities as a writer? It also seems that, both in the dream as a whole as well as in the small events that followed it in the morning, everything was so arranged as to emphasize the progressive development of the idea of the square or rectangle: implicitly introduced by the roughly hewn block of stone, it becomes more evident with the balcony surrounding the nave or lobby, is further accentuated by the jube-banquet table and, upon waking, is finally concretized by the breakfast tray. There is also a certain schoolish element to the dream, immediately apparent by the presence of an old schoolmate of mine, which perhaps provides the key to its construction. Its structure, which could strike one as derived from an arithmetic or geometry lesson, is schoolish, as is its content: the erudite mention of the crypts of Lalibala, an allusion to the new field of knowledge I had just begun specializing in; the high-schoolish episode with the jube (probably a deformed image of a reproduction of the jube of Saint-Etienne-du-Mont glimpsed in some history textbook); the grade-schoolish evocation of Notre-Dame and the Sainte-Chapelle (which I believe our older sister made my brother and me visit, along with other Parisian monuments, so that our days off from school would at least serve some educational purpose).

An analysis of this sort is, of course, not without its risks and at any rate can only account for a small portion of the facts. But perhaps this kind of analysis offers the means, as it were, to *solidify* the dream by providing it with a certain logic and by erasing the gap between life and dream through the discovery of their common roots—just as I had discovered among the tea cups cluttered on our breakfast tray a prolongation of the dream sequence in which I was unwilling to let a single drop of coffee go to waste.

September, 1933

By a pool, a row of giant toads the size of chimpanzees, all covered with moss. They would appear to be part gorilla, and their colors range from green to gray to brown. The finest specimen—to the extreme left of the row—is bottle-green with huge eyes like frosted lightbulbs. They are all getting ready to dive into the water and crawl back into their shells (?) It occurs to me that if I dressed up in knickerbockers and wore a large green felt cap, I would look like a toad.

October 8-9, 1933

President Lebrun has died and the new head of state is to be Louis Barthou. Nighttime Paris is bustling with events related to the official funeral ceremonies: floodlights (such as I saw as a child, probably on the occasion of the visit of some foreign sovereign); twenty-one gun salutes; troops moving from one place to another; an atmosphere of general mobilization; silent panic spreading through the crowd. The profoundly *funereal* look of the President's morning coat (suggestive of a dummy in a shop window).

Drawing a conclusion from all of the above, I am about to deliver some definitive pronouncement on the subject of anxiety when Z . . . wakes me up, informing me that I am on the verge of screaming.

Undated

A ceremonial reception by an exotic monarch. The reception takes place in a theater; my mother and my wife are in the audience.

From the stage, someone calls out my name: it is my turn to be received. I climb a few steps and make my way onto the stage. A river to be crossed, flowing between two rows of grandstands, like some water tower. On the other side, a pride of panthers and leopards (not visible, yet I am convinced they will come at me). I reassure myself momentarily by reflecting that this is simply my imagination: in fact, it's nothing but a large leopard skin.

The potentate sits on a very high throne, hidden from sight. One or two men guard the stairs that lead up to the area where the audience will take place; they resemble monkeys and wear death's-head masks—for a moment I wonder if I shouldn't be wearing the same kind of mask. The backdrop of this stage by the stairs remains ill-defined, almost invisible, merely hinted at. I have left my gloves and overcoat in the safekeeping of my mother and my wife. I go up a spiral staircase. When I get to the top I meet a guard dressed in khaki and wearing a visored cap (somewhat like the Addis Ababa policemen I saw in Ethiopia). I ask the guard where the audience will be taking place, while realizing I have taken the wrong stairs. The stairs I should have taken run exactly parallel to these and lead up a ramp they both share. I am about to cross over this ramp when the guard stops me, informing me that because of my error I must now humbly wait my turn to be received. He leads me to a chamber where I take off my overcoat (which I am therefore still wearing at that point). I am mortified at the thought that the sovereign must be waiting for me.

At the end of a hallway I catch sight of an Arab dressed in European fashion and who turns out to be a barber. He is conversing with an elderly gentleman, Semitic in appearance, dressed like a bedouin, whose face is emaciated. At moments his face seems veiled to me and perhaps the man has two heads, one uncovered (that he holds high as he faces me), the other wrapped in cloth (that he presents to me bowed and in profile). I wait and wait. My name is not called. I assume that I have missed my turn and leave.

Once outside, I realize that I have forgotten my overcoat but do not dare return to the palace to retrieve it. I walk until I reach a courtyard—the courtyard of my own house. As I enter it, I meet a camel and notice that it indeed has two humps, which strikes me as irrefutable proof that the word "camel" applies to the double-humped creature and not to the single-humped creature, which is in fact a dromedary. Brownish in color, the camel prances about and calls out to me with glee. Rearing up, it reaches out one of its forelegs to shake my hand. The brownish color of its coat as well as the vulgarity of its cordiality convince me that if I shake its hand, mine will be sullied by some sort of filth or excrement. But at the camel's insistence we end up slapping palms, executing the traditional gesture that accompanies the expression, "It's a deal!"

March, 1934

I am wearing a colonial helmet fashioned out of heavy mahogany that I brought back from Africa. The helmet is most handsome but its chin strap is nearly broken.

I feel quite uneasy upon waking, interpreting the chin strap as a symbol of castration.

March, 1934

I am traveling through a country, which may be Ethiopia or Mexico, in the company of a very young woman with whom, in my waking life, I am in love.

At the end of that particular day's journey, we stop for the night in a small castle surrounded by a huge park. Our host, who physically resembles the vampire in the German film *Nosferatu*, keeps a supply of young girls on hand in several hunting lodges for his eventual debaucheries. At nightfall, he summons from the deer park the girl (or girls) he wants to sleep with, and for that purpose, befitting his refined libertine tastes, he dispatches a coach hitched to horses decked out in colors that vary according to the girl (or girls) he happens to desire. That night we see a coach drawn by two horses, one black, the other white, and we understand that he is lusting after the two sisters we have come to protect (which leads to various subsequent events whose scenario remains utterly vague).

Other travels follow, but my young woman friend is no longer on the scene. I am walking through a town whose streets are steep and rocky, escorted by Francis Poulenc (who is merely a presence, totally independent of the fact that he is a musician or that he has co-authored the ballet *Les Biches* with the mellow colorist Marie Laurencin). He himself is flanked by a young boy whom he is familiarly holding by the hand. I am exhausted, my feet hurt, I have difficulty following my two companions, I am exhausted . . .

Finally I find myself on a seashore where I may be vacationing, and am exploring the rocks with two other companions: my mother, as she is in real life, and one of my older brothers who is still a small boy. I am lagging behind them and this fact humiliates me. They are cheerfully clambering up a steep slope. I am delighted to discover a vaulted passageway that will enable me to catch up with them without too much difficulty.

March, 1934

I find myself on the upper deck of a bus, an elevated balustrade of sorts that moves through the streets. Leaning far over the railing, I keep my feet planted on a bar that is a separate apparatus capable of independent movement but that runs parallel to the guard rail above it.

I realize that I am in a dangerous position and that the slightest jolt could catapult me over the side. I decide to get down, only to find myself in a rather narrow stairway that is pitching like a boat; to each side lies the ocean. Losing my balance at every point, I end up going down the stairs the safest way possible—on the seat of my pants. When I get to the bottom I am now in a boat—still pitching—making my way through a lock. I lie down flat on my stomach and feel the lapping of the waves. The boat then becomes a naked woman (someone I know) and I am lying on this woman, caressing her breasts.

The dream ends, literally, with an emission.

March, 1934

The theatrical spectacle in question may just as well be a music hall performance or an opera, a comedy or a drama.

One corner of the scenery—quite luminous and distinct—features a hammock slung high up on a wall. It initially makes me think of a net and then, because of the curve of its contour, of a siren arching her loins . . . I then see a large set of stairs which a very powerful revolutionary choir is majestically ascending.

A few weeks prior to this dream—February 12—was I not an atom in the large crowd that witnessed, between the Place de la République and Nation, the coming together of two processions—one communist, the other socialist—to symbolically mark their unification within the Popular Front?

March 27-28, 1934

I am with a woman close to my heart, on board a boat, about to disembark, perhaps for a simple call at port, accompanied by Z . . . and several other acquaintances who are traveling in our party. Searching for a doll my lady friend has just lost (just as several days ago she had lost her pocketbook at an actual ball we were attending), I comb the stairways and the parlors amid the crush of passengers. Meet a little girl (barely pubescent and probably related to that girl whose spunk so struck me when I gave that lecture-tour at the Trocadero Museum of Ethnography for a group of teenagers who belonged to the left-wing youth group, "The Red Falcons"). The doll the little girl is holding is the one I'm looking for, so I ask her for it. She gives it to me, proud to have found the lost item. I chat with her, we disembark together, and walk along the pier.

The little girl seems to enjoy my company greatly, and I notice that she is quite developed for her age (she's probably 12 or 13). After a while, it occurs to me that she's probably spent a fair amount of time with me by now: her parents are going to start worrying and wondering what on earth I am doing with her. So I tell her she'll get into trouble with her parents if she doesn't leave right away. She then explains to me that she is studying dance and, growing ever more flirtatious, she overtly sets out to seduce me.

I am now in a room, either in a hotel or a private apartment, to which I have been led by the young ballerina who soon becomes identified with the woman who had lost the doll (a woman whom I see almost on a daily basis without any need to dream and whose young daughter I know). The girl-woman or the woman-girl—subsequently confused with Z . . . and no longer with her rival—had made preparations for a sort of bacchanalia: two sailors are present, along with two prostitutes, all four of them getting ready to make love at the same time, but without promiscuity. Things get delayed a bit. One makes sure that all the doors are shut tight. Then I get undressed and start, I believe, not by taking off my jacket (as I do in real life), but by dropping my trousers right away. At which point a door that we had not noticed opens: one of my three sisters-in-law, a spinster, enters, bringing a hot-water bottle or some other item of domestic comfort to my wife. The woman-girl and I are horribly embarrassed at having been surprised in the company of couples about to engage in group sex.

A detail of the interior decoration: a sort of wardrobe, tall and narrow, featuring three circular apertures in a vertical row which have been installed for voyeurs or which are themselves the heads of voyeurs. Several pistol shots are aimed at this wardrobe, probably by the sailors.

March 29-30, 1934

Caravan in Africa, traveling with this young woman I'm obsessed by, along with her daughter and a man (whom I admire in real life without knowing him well and who lives in Dahomey) who is romantically linked to the young woman. We are rolling along on unicycles of sorts whose handlebars are so extraordinarily low that our heads are almost at the level of our feet. Since the road is poor and not suitable for this mode of locomotion, we frequently fall off. We find ourselves on a difficult, muddy stretch which we climb on foot. Having decided with puritanical obstinacy that she should display all the energy which she is capable of despite her small build, the man accompanying my female friend makes no effort to help her. So she struggles onward with difficulty, holding her little girl around the waist or thighs as she pushes or carries her forward. Perhaps as an act of protest against this man who is walking ahead of us as if he were our leader, I place myself behind my friend and help her along, holding her the same way she is holding her little girl (this little girl who comes to her mother's bed to snuggle up and who one day told her she *loved her skin,* or so the mother informed me during one of our actual conversations). Then the road levels out again, the ground still muddy and its contact still disagreeable as we make our way over it barefooted, the puritan and I.

At our stopover point, games are being organized around the campfires. All the men, myself included, are wearing soccer outfits. Among the participants is my old friend Abba Jérôme Gabra Moussié (the Abyssinian scholar who acted as my interpreter while I was studying the beliefs surrounding possession at Gandor, in Ethiopia). We form a large circle and execute a round dance holding hands.

Then these collective celebrations turn into a political demonstration not unlike those that took place in February. I take part in it as a member of the Croix de Feu (even though I in fact have nothing in common with them from a political point of view). We make our way to the Chambre des Députés—or to some other government building—knowing that the guardsmen will shoot to kill. For me it is a question of putting my courage to the test and of discovering just what my attitude will be when the shooting starts and the wounded start dropping. All the demonstrators have their right arms raised; densely packed together and staggered at different heights, these arms form an ascending series of organ stops or Panpipe reeds. All this takes place in front of an art deco monument illuminated by one or more klieg lights.

Through a simple glass door watched over by a man in a museum guard's uniform, we leave the area of the demonstration and find ourselves in front of a department store of the "Old England" style. On exhibit in one of its aisles—the "Dahomy aisle"—is a wax head supposedly representing a horse-guard. Wearing some sort of sealskin hat, the head has long, droopy reddish moustaches that evoke the typical British tourist wearing his cap and Inverness cape.

April 2-3, 1934

This woman I am in love with and I are following our story in an illustrated weekly for children. Each week we buy a new installment and both in the little blocks of print and in the accompanying illustrations, we discover descriptions of everything we will be doing.

May 8-9, 1934

This same very young woman and I appear at a school, no doubt in order to enroll as students. It is a villa with a garden. We are ushered into some sort of circular straw hut with a conical roof (such as I have seen in Sudan): a kennel where dogs of every species lie in the straw. A porter (?), probably black, wearing a uniform and a sailor's cap, tells us it is here that we will live. We will have to sleep *beneath* the dogs.

May 14-15, 1934

In England, packing my bags to take a boat later that morning. Unable to locate the suitcase I need to store all my belongings in. But in fact I'm not too worried: I do not know exactly at what time the ship will weigh anchor, but I am almost certain it will not leave without me. A stroll through the countryside along a river where there is a regatta going on. Various boats are racing in the direction of the sea. There are motorboats and vessels made of empty red wine bottles equipped with outboard engines (liter bottles straddled by the competitors which, seen from afar, are equivalent in volume to real liter bottles seen close up).

As for us, we will be at the tiller of a hydroplane that will brave the ocean waves. We are walking through fields so abundantly irrigated that it seems as if we are wading up a torrent.

June 29-30, 1934

Upon leaving some ceremony that (probably) took place at the Trocadéro Museum of Ethnography, I run into a famous psychoanalyst who is also a Princess and whom I had seen two or three days earlier in real life. She berated me for my book *L'Afrique fantôme* (published in April), noting my "masochistic passivity." When I meet her in my dream, she takes my right hand, sinks her teeth into the phalanx of my bent index finger and remains in that position for some time as she walks and talks with me. She invites me to visit her at home so she can continue to give me her opinion of my travel journal. I consult my appointment calendar but find I am booked up.

In the course of the official events of the evening, a film about a composer was shown. The young hero of the film, an Austrian officer with a moustache, outfitted in a short military jacket decorated with frogs and loops, was singing a song that contained the word "Marcade." A contraction of the word "marquise" and of the supposed name of a flower, this word brought to mind (even before I awoke) the two main characters in a play by Roger Vitrac: Arcade and Désirade, the protagonists—one male, the other female—of his *Coup de Trafalgar*. The song is a satirical ditty that makes fun of the composer. The lyrics are translated for me: "When he directs, put him in slow motion," a phrase that was in fact addressed to the crew that shot the film, inducing them to engage in some sort of sabotage or practical joke that will victimize the musician who supposedly was to be honored.

The Same Night

Boulevard de Grenelle beneath the elevated tracks, I hear a worker talking about the 1914-18 war: "A company wiped out by a storm . . . Whenever the subject came up—Oh, those poor old guys! It sure wasn't no storm . . ." A pause. Then: "As long as they're not about to start another war."

November 24-25, 1934

I am walking around Paris with a friend, then go to the Bois de Boulogne with an adult lion that belongs to our common friend Marcel Moré (whose hair, although cropped short, always reminded me of a lion's mane). At some point, I give the lion a few hard slaps that literally *smash* his face. The lion takes it without reacting. I burst out laughing at his docility.

At some other point, I am traveling around on a streetcar. I hope that our route will cross that of a man condemned to death who is to be led to the gallows or the electric chair. I know for a fact that he will follow custom by sprinting from the prison to the place of execution; his performance will be clocked and he will attempt to break the record.

Undated

A tiny gray cat facing off against a mouse (or some other rodent) exactly its size. These two creatures locked in combat are in reality a single bird with a large, almost pelican-like beak (etched in silhouette or an armature of steel wire, slightly downy or bearded), a bird more or less reduced to its lineaments, scabby, busy eating its plumage that has just gone up in flames. Grotesque image of a phoenix that has turned transparent after having fed on its own pyre.

Undated

It has been agreed that as soon as the 1937 Exposition opens I will take my young niece Germaine Lascaux there to see a performance of *Carmen*. Instead of the bullfight that is occasionally tacked on to the last act (in open-air performances in the arena of Arles or elsewhere), there will be the following attraction: an animal trainer working at a typewriter with his back turned to his wild beasts.

Awaking, I realize that the trainer-typist (a substitute matador) is myself. Dozing off again to discover the word he is typing on his machine is: *Public Opinion*.

Summer 1939

(real-life)

"I am the Volcano . . . ," a bearded man on the pier announces by way of introduction. We have just landed on Santorini. Its volcano, very active at the moment, rises out of the water in the center of the nearly perfect ring that constitutes the inhabited portion of the island.

The individual who has thus announced himself (we almost had to pinch ourselves to make sure we weren't dreaming) is a Frenchman whose beard is of a very rich color, although not quite flaming red. He turns out to be the proprietor of the Volcano Hotel, which is where we end up staying. During dinner, having partaken of "Vulcanic Port Wine," we play our little part in a domestic farce whose major scenes take place in the wings: the proprietor of the hotel accuses his daughter of being a slut (she must have stayed out all night or have gotten pregnant), the mother wails, the girl gets fresh, the father rants and raves, periodically interrupting his performance to come into the dining room to see if we are satisfied with our meal.

Before dinner, we have no trouble finding a boat to take us to the erupting volcano, even though the area has been placed off-limits by the authorities. We walk around the tiny island; the water surrounding it is very hot and the island itself is grumbling and sputtering. We feel the burning ground underfoot and, somewhat apprehensive, observe the crevasses, the lava, and the eruptions of sulphur all around us. All this naturally makes us think of the war which, from the stray bits of news we hear, seems all the more threatening.

We decide to beat a quick retreat: there is a rumbling underground more powerful than anything we've heard so far and it is so close to us that we feel it—or believe we feel it—right under our feet.

June 1940

(real-life)

Yesterday evening a number of other soldiers and I unexpectedly left the Palais de la Mutualité, the depot where our company was more or less camping out. We were being transferred to some unknown destination in the same fashion that, without even leaving one's bed, one can set off at night in the direction of dream (*rêve* with a capital R which expresses its royal majesty and its romanticism à la *René*) or of nightmare (whether it grunts like a pig or snores like someone sleeping).

As we return from our mission (which had taken us into some vague region of the southeastern suburbs, to the storage dump of the chemical weapons that had been evacuated from Laon to keep them from falling into the hands of the advancing German motorized divisions), there is an air-raid alert that holds up the train in the Melun station. We all have to take cover in the cellars of the Brasserie Grüber, whose metallic

107

decor evokes some ancient foundry or gallery of machines rather than a place where hops are fermenting into ale. Once the alert is over, we make our way back to the station where a number of retreating civilians are waiting with their various suitcases and packages.

Holding a black cat on her knees, an elderly lady exchanges grievances with another woman. As she was about to leave home, there had been a problem involving her pets: there was no difficulty in taking her cat along, but what to do with the goldfish? Unwilling to encumber herself with the fishbowl, yet unwilling to abandon its occupant, the woman solved the problem by feeding the fish to the cat.

As I look at the cat—nice and plump, with shiny fur—I realize that, in contrast to his owner who had made such a fuss about having to deal with the harsh necessities of war, this cat thinks he has at last accomplished what had long been the dream of his life, the very thing he had been lying in wait for day after day, pretending to be mesmerized.

July 12, 1940

(real-life)

Waiting to be demobbed in Lot-et-Garonne where my wife has rejoined me after the chaotic exodus from Paris, I visit a church at Mauvezin (near Lagupie) whose facade has been half destroyed by lightning (I have no idea how long ago). Of its two bells, only one still functions; the other has come loose and nests in its alveolus as though suspended in the open sky.

In the church, my wife and I glimpse the back of a soldier who is playing a harmonium and whose appearance would seem to suggest he is a priest. Even though he appears to have heard us, he does not turn around. A kind of wooden baptismal font, standing free like a desk and placed several meters away from the entrance, has a sign propped up on it that reads DANGER. And indeed, a length of steel wire has been strung across the church, prohibiting access to its front portion. This is where we had entered, unaware that this part of the church (as well as its facade) was

109

in danger of collapsing. In the peristyle, a heap of bees, many dead, others still abuzz. It's rainy out and we also notice some bees drowned in a puddle. Other bees, some dead, some still alive, are scattered throughout the building. Is this some swarm the wind has ravaged?

Cypress trees have been planted around the church, a common sight in this region. Facing the tombs, a large Christ with his back to the wall.

After he has finished playing, the soldier shuts the harmonium and leaves. Once outside, he grabs a wheelbarrow which appears to be empty and, pushing it in front of him, races off with it as though he were escaping with some stolen object or had suddenly been struck with panic. The truth is probably that he is in a hurry to find shelter, for it appears that it is about to rain again.

July 12-13, 1940

(Lagupie)

Waking up (with a shriek that Z . . . muffles) from the following dream: as if to catch a glimpse of something, I insert my head into an opening that resembles an oeil-de-boeuf window overlooking a dark, enclosed area akin to those cylindrical pisé granary lofts that I saw in black Africa between 1931 and 1933 and also reminiscent of those covered alleyways in certain neighborhoods of Oran that I visited when I was a soldier in the South during the "phoney war."

My anxiety derives from the fact that as I lean over this enclosed area and get a glimpse of its inner darkness, I am actually gazing into myself.

January 29-30, 1941

(*Boulogne-Billancourt*)

After a quarrel with Z . . ., a major fit of despair. Bursting into tears, somewhat theatrically but none-theless sincerely, as though this represented the only way out, a solution that took virtually no effort on my part. The idea of a life that has been totally wasted, a life (like any life) doomed to be utterly devoid of meaning, utterly wasted (and this independent of historical circumstances and the fact I am living in occupied territory).

I owned a crystal sword (similar to that life-size, 18th-century glass sword I saw at Robert Desnos's place a number of years ago). In a fit of rage, I hurled this sword (of which I was especially fond) to the ground in the hope of breaking it. The sword would not break. To punish me for my fit of anger (and knowing that deep down I had no desire to break the sword and that my gesture was purely theatrical), Z . . . took hold of the crystal weapon and in turn attempted to break it on the ground. Hence the quarrel, hence my despair.

112

November 3-4, 1941

(Boulogne-Billancourt)

I am eating or smoking opium with Z . . . and several other people who are our close friends. Gradually it seems to me that everybody's hands—including mine—have turned very white. Which leads me to conclude that we have just crossed the slippery, dizzying threshold of dream. This causes me considerable anxiety.

March 3, 1942

(*real-life, Boulogne-Billancourt*)

While sitting up at night in the library which is heated by a stove and has practically become our living room, an air-raid alert. The fascinating spectacle of the sky lit up with anti-aircraft flares. Novices, we gawk as if it were all a fine display of fireworks and, without missing a beat, we follow the merry-go-round of airplanes which we initially take to be the German defenses, unaware that this apocalyptic glare is not meant to detect attacking planes but rather to blind their approach to their bombing targets. Explosions over toward the Renault factories. Then a lull, during which my sister-in-law and our young blonde-haired maid retire for the night, leaving my wife and me alone in the library, a room on the ground floor which opens out into the garden. The calm is far from complete, but I force myself to read—as if nothing were happening—a novel by Robert Louis Stevenson, translated into French under the title *Le Reflux.*

Just as I am coming to one of the most crucial episodes in the book—a schooner suddenly bursting into flames—all hell breaks loose: the window thrown open amid a shatter of glass, a gust of wind dislodging the stove and showering dust and sparks all over the room. A number of ear-splitting shrieks are let out by our young maid (a dumb, incompetent, but not unpleasant girl who would leave our service shortly thereafter and who, as we later found out, would become a stripper or something of that sort in a girlie show on the outskirts of Paris). We rush up to the second floor to find its two inhabitants safe and sound. Since I am the only male on the scene, I take command of the situation and order everybody down into the cellar.

Shortly before midnight, the air-raid alert ends and we leave the underground shelter where we had been shivering, not from the cold (as we had believed) but from fear. The damage to the house seemed to be limited: some broken panes of glass, the ironwork and hinges of the windows all twisted, broken locks and bolts on the front and cellar doors, plaster strewn in the downstairs hallway. It was only afterwards that we would notice one of the dividing walls had a crack running through it.

I have a look outdoors and am surprised to find the rue de l'Ancienne-Mairie littered with fallen shutters, shards of glass, and debris of all kinds; on the corner where yesterday an apartment building 7 or 8 stories tall stood, there are now ruins and a huge fire. We pick our way through the chaos. Wearing a pair of old patent leather shoes (which I would put on every evening when I came home in order to save my other shoes from wear), dressed in a large double-breasted navy suit (which I had ordered at the "Petit Matelot" when times were beginning to get rough), I feel absolutely preposterous—a foreign body, as in those dreams where the sleeper's nightclothes are transformed into some incongruous mode of dress—and I think of an American film that was shown in Paris a number of years before the war: it featured Clark Gable, dressed in a black suit, wandering through the fissures and debris of the famous earthquake that destroyed San Francisco.

The aftermath: six hundred dead and two thousand wounded in our district, according to morning rumors.

March 28-29, 1942

(Boulogne-Billancourt)

Z . . ., some friends and I are all vacationing in a town by the sea which is at once a port and a resort (reminiscent of Le Havre which is being bombed with frequency these days and about which I had been talking yesterday evening at a gathering cut short by an air-raid alert).

A life of pleasure pre-war style. There is a casino or nightclub with an excellent negro band; we are buddies with the band members, just the way it used to be possible to strike up friendships with the Blackbirds or other black artists in the music halls. There are lots of people there, whites as well as blacks, and they are dancing so well that out of modesty I punctiliously abstain from venturing onto the dance floor. Georges Limbour turns up (currently teaching philosophy at Dieppe). He informs me that the coffin-boats have just pulled into port; these boats are used to transport the corpses of the people who live by the

117

sea, people who are something more than sailors because they live *on* the sea roughly the same way that gypsies or tramps live on the road. Seeing my astonishment at these coffin-boats, Limbour explains to me that it is altogether natural that the corpses of those who live on the sea should be transported in boats, just as the corpses of those who live on land are transported in coffins. Night is falling. Limbour suggests we go take a look at the boats before it gets too dark.

We make our way to the harbor, a small fishing port with a stone wharf with steps leading downward. The coffin-boats are lying at anchor; they are pirogues of sorts, hewn out of hollowed tree trunks (an ethnographic reminiscence suggested—as were the negroes—by the fact that yesterday I was in the process of drinking white rum when we suddenly had to take shelter in the basement?). Fish are laid out on the steps leading down to the docks. They appear to be rotting. Limbour explains to me that this makes little difference, seeing as these fish are food for the dead. He proposes we go get a closer look at the boats in order to find out if they contain any corpses. I decline his invitation and he proceeds on his own toward one of the hollowed trunks. I see him lift up a tarpaulin that covers a dead man stretched out full length in the boat. Deep down, I feel that he is exaggerating a bit, that he is pushing his curiosity beyond the bounds of common decency, but I recognize this impiety, this romantic irreverence as being entirely in character.

From that moment on, the dream unravels. Final episode: another friend who is also on the scene (Jean-Baptiste Piel?, a native of Le Havre like Limbour and recently released from prison camp) takes a child's bicycle he has found on the docks, pushes it up the steps, hops on it, and executes a few turns in front of a number of people who admire his skill, for it is rather difficult for an adult to ride a bicycle this tiny.

May 19-20, 1942

Condemned to death by the Germans, I take the thing manfully enough until I am told that they are going to come give me a shave in the early afternoon— a final grooming before my execution. Having concentrated all my attention on this final grooming, I had lost sight of the ultimate fact of my execution. But now that I know the hour at which it will take place, my mind can move beyond it, and the screen which had been placed between death and myself by this detail of protocol now disappears. As there is no longer anything separating me from my execution, my courage gives way to undescribable anguish. I feel I will not be able to face up to the ordeal, that I will be led to the stake kicking and screaming.

I subsequently dream about the publication of the memoirs of my colleague at the Musée de l'Homme, Anatole Lewitzky (who was in fact shot by the Germans on February 23rd of this year). Noting all the last-minute impressions of a man condemned to death, he tells how the execution took place on some abandoned fairgrounds at the foot of the Mont Valé-rien. He was lined up with his friends with his back against a reconstructed African roundhouse made of pisé or dried clay. Lewitzky reports that in front of the door of the hut that was serving as an execution stake, there was a chicken or the skeleton of a chicken on the ground (like those feathers of sacrificially slaughtered chickens or those animal skulls or jawbones that one sees on household altars in Africa). He closes with a kind of political testament or credo: rallying cries, confident predictions as to the outcome of the war.

One Week Later

The friends and relatives of Anatole Lewitzky have been given permission to visit him just before his execution. I set out to see him, terrified that I will arrive too late, but as I have always loathed running, I slacken my pace after a few meters.

I find Lewitzky in a large room, surrounded by most of the people who work at the Trocadéro Museum. Under his floppy hat, his face with its slightly Mongol eyes and cheekbones strikes me as extremely pale (but no paler, in fact, than it usually was). I embrace him in tears. As a farewell gift, one of the museum staff offers him an enormous bowl of steaming soup. Very calmly, he sniffs the vapor of the soup and agrees to partake of it in our presence while we all stand around him (as if for some religious ceremony), deeply moved.

In 1955 I will rediscover something of the atmosphere of this dream and the preceding dream when, upon visiting the Cultural Palace of the Workers in Shanghai on October 12th, I see the series of photos depicting the revolutionary hero Wang Hsiao-ho, a worker at the central electric power-station who was shot by the Kuomintang. One of the photos shows him at his trial—young, handsome, smiling. Another photo shows him striding toward his death, showering prophetic invectives on the reactionary government.

Undated

(morning dream, Saint-Léonard de Noblat)

I go through the motions of taking off a pair of glasses (even though my eyes had no need of them at that period). This gesture of removing something I am wearing in front of my eyes constitutes the moment of awakening, as if it corresponded to the real action I perform when opening my lids.

August 28-29, 1942

(morning dream, Saint-Léonard de Noblat)

I am the actor Jean Yonnel and I am declaiming a
Racinian sort of tragedy. Suddenly I no longer remember my lines. Speaking slowly in short jerky sentences,
though still maintaining my declamatory fervor, I
proclaim that because present circumstances have
made me become conscious of tragedy, I can no longer
perform tragedy as I used to, a performance which
only my lack of awareness had made possible.

Beyond the moral significance of this theme (tragedy as an art form devalued by the living experience of
tragedy), there is also the way in which this theme is
linked to the very process of awaking: as I regain
consciousness (that is, as I leave sleep behind), I
discover myself incapable of reciting my lines (or more
precisely: I discover that I was only imagining myself
to be reciting). Asleep, I recited or imagined myself
reciting lines (to be exact: though I was saying
nothing, I was nonetheless in the same emotional state

125

as someone reciting his lines); but upon waking (already half-conscious), discovering that I will truly have to invent my lines instead of merely acting as if I were reciting them, I come up with a compromise. I continue to speak, but only in order to speak about speaking my lines.

One of my most powerful memories of the stage is Yonnel playing Orestes in *Andromaque,* his style of acting at once vehement and decorous, making use of every modulation of his fine voice. I remember leaving the theater, still in that heightened state every spectacle ought to induce in us, and being horribly upset that I had to deal with the crush of the subway and the hassles at the ticket booth because of some error I had made in small change. I railed against this obligatory return to my senses; I had been bathing in a myth, and in a split-second it had all evaporated.

September 8-9, 1942

(Saint-Léonard de Noblat)

On a tomb (mine?) someone has affixed a sign providing an epitaph that condenses the life of the deceased
into a few lines. The sign is entitled "ARGUMENT."

127

November 21-22, 1942

Shortly before changing subway lines (most likely at the Motte-Piquet station), I am hastily polishing off some food (meat with noodles and vegetables) in a metal plate that I leave, once I'm done with it, on one of the seats in the second class compartment. I am standing among a group of workers who—displaying the same gluttony we all shared at that point—had been eating off plates similar to mine but who were alert enough to have finished their food by the time the train pulled into the station. As for me, the train has already come to a stop and I am still gulping down the last bites. In addition, I still have to gather up my hat, my raincoat, my suitcase and some other item that must be the hood of a raincoat that belongs to Z . . . No time to pack the latter (as well as the other items perhaps?) into the suitcase. So I just grab everything I can and get off.

It turns out I am not changing subway lines but changing trains and I find myself outside in the open air, waiting on a platform in a train station. It will no doubt be a fairly long time before my train arrives. It occurs to me that I could get rid of my bags by checking them, so I decide to redo them and, more specifically, to pack away the hood. In order to open the suitcase, I take my keys from my pocket. The suitcase is open; I arrange the items in it; all I need to do now is close it. The keys fall to the ground (which is very sandy or dusty) and vanish as if swallowed up. I nonetheless manage to retrieve most of them, but notice they are broken, twisted, useless. I must have destroyed them while trying to get the suitcase open. I am quite upset: how am I going to close the thing again? Worse yet, I now realize that I have lost a tiny key which I obviously don't need right at the moment but that I'll need when I get back home. Everything would have been far simpler, I wouldn't have lost anything if instead of having carried the keys loose in my pocket I had attached them all to a chain as is my usual habit. With no great sense of hope I dig around a bit in the dusty soil. I initially come up with a small steel key, quite modern in design, composed solely of a cylindrical stem and a notched bit, but lacking a loop. How on earth could I get the thing to work? Then I examine an object that I absolutely do not recognize and that was no doubt lost by some previous traveler. It is a pipe bowl made of sculpted ivory and carved into a Christ's head surrounded by a halo.

February 28-March 1, 1943

I go to a place that resembles both the old 45 rue
Blomet (now rebuilt, but where André Masson and
Joan Miró used to have their studios) and 54 rue du
Château (a small townhouse shared by Jacques Prévert,
Yves Tanguy, and Marcel Duhamel). There are one or
more courtyards in the place, with a number of studios
on the ground floor. I am supposed to be meeting a
group of people who have gathered there for cocktails
or for a more or less "hep" dance party. Just as the party
is about to begin, I find myself with one of the guests
in one of the studios, a sort of shed with a hard dirt
floor. All of a sudden my friend throws himself to the
ground and recommends I do likewise. He informs me
that the occupation authorities have just posted the
following message all over Paris: "Hit the ground or
say your prayers," thereby ordering the entire population of Paris to lie down on the spot under penalty of
death. The Allies have just unleashed their attack: this
is the final fight to the death. Patrols will be checking

130

every house and will shoot on sight anybody who has not obeyed the order. My friend and I lie there grovelling, our faces flush to the ground.

March 19-20, 1943

The dream I'm in the middle of begins to resemble a state of waking that is about to end: unable to resist falling asleep in the dream itself, I sense that this dream is about to conclude, not with a return to reality but with a plunge into the void of unconsciousness. I prepare myself to cry out in fright, but Z . . . intervenes and my uneasiness ceases.

A movement analogous to the one that often tends to elicit similar screams from me just as I am about to awake. But in this case the movement was considerably more frightening; instead of those interminable pangs one experiences when emerging with difficulty from a dream, I was in a sense being precipitated downward by my dream, plunged into a sleep from which I would never escape, and which would be my death.

April 7-8, 1943

Standing beneath some sort of terrace (or aqueduct? water, after all, is being channeled through it), I am examining a statue made out of iron or sheet metal, a religious object from some distant land that resembles the shop signs or weathervanes found in our own country. The statue is equipped with a series of accessories also made of iron (roughly the size of a series of charms on a bracelet). I surmise they represent the rosary of islands visited by Ulysses. These variously shaped objects are attached at an equal distance along the length of a single chain. I let this chain or rosary drop into the water channel (a kind of open gutter). I will therefore have to fish it out again.

The scene has now changed. I am in a huge sunken hall whose floor is situated far below ground level, thus creating a cellar-like penumbra (the dim lighting of an old engraving); through the openings of the overhead vault (a kind of church vault, constructed in the bizarre, anachronistic style of Saint-Eustache), one can see the sun filter in. To my right, the hall widens

133

into an immense grotto whose entrance is half-obstructed by large strands of hanging ivy similar to those curtains of glass beads or metal mesh found in the doorways of many shops or homes of southern France and whose function is to keep flies out of the house. Through this hall flows the water channel (or sewer) into which I must dip my hand. I roll up the sleeves of my shirt and jacket to avoid getting dirty. The idea of blindly digging around in this mud disgusts me. I am afraid that my hand will come into contact with some unnameable creature or object. And indeed, as I begin feeling around I touch something alive; it is a toad so coated with mud that it is almost shapeless. Then I pull several little metal chains out of the slime, but not the chain I was looking for. Continuing to dig around with my left hand (which is the hand I'm using, as though it were somehow more hygienic to get my left hand dirty than my right), I take some sort of earthworm or slender snake between my fingers and lift it from the slime. At which point someone informs me that this worm or snake is "German" (in the full sense of the adjective: that is, designating a citizen of Germany and not just something that belongs to the Germans, as does everything in this hall, located as it is in occupied territory). Because I have not yet managed to retrieve the objects I am looking for, I will have to go on digging, a prospect I look upon with disgust and alarm, for God knows what intolerably sordid discovery I will next unearth in this hall whose interior suggests some enormous alchemical athanor and that contains a grotto whose blackness opens the secret abysses of nature right by my side, leaving me separated from the antechamber of death by little more than a vague doorway of dusty leaves.

134

May 4, 1943

(real-life)

Leaving work and about to take the métro at the Trocadéro station, I see a man lurking in the corridor that leads from the stairs of the subway entrance on the Passy side of the Palais de Chaillot to the rotunda where they sell tickets and newspapers. He is more or less middle-aged, flushed and corpulent, sporting a gray hat, and his handlebar moustache is so strikingly brown (if not entirely black) that I wonder for a moment whether it might not be fake. Walking by this figure who seems to be too perfect a caricature of a cop, I am gripped by a bizarre sensation: the same fear that Mardi Gras masks used to cause me when I was a child.

A real cop or a mere civilian? Or nobody in particular? I asked myself the question but could not resist considering this shady character to be some sort of specter or macabre merrymaker who, having donned a terrifyingly contemporary disguise, was waiting for some shadowy carnival to begin.

May 16-17, 1944

I am to be executed because I am a member of the
resistance or a hostage or because of some entirely
different reason, and this fact occasions a sort of fiesta
on the part of my friends. I say my goodbyes to Z . . .,
most heartrending. I also say farewell to one of our
friends whom I am very fond of—Simone de Beau-
voir—or I am looking for her in order to say goodbye.
No guards around me; I appear to be completely free.
My friends are lined up in front of me two deep, like
a crowd at the finish line of the Tour de France, and
I pass by them accompanied by Z . . . who is escorting
me as though I were a child that needed reassurance.
We arrive at a wall of rock, irregular in shape and
pocked by bullets, where the execution is to take place;
I place my back against it with Z . . . still by my side
(to my right, I believe, squeezing my hand). I jam my
back to the wall as hard as I can, as if I were trying
to embed myself into it, not so much in order to
disappear into it as to muster in myself some of its
rigidity—not physical, but moral rigidity, in other

words, courage. I hear horses and perhaps the sound of marching troops. Sinking into abject terror, I feel all my bravado melt away. Then I grow furious and tell Z . . . that I'm not going to let myself be killed like this. Then I scurry off and plunge headlong into a sunken alley that runs parallel to the row of our spectator friends. The fall awakens me, or rather takes me into another dream in which I am explaining to someone the way I manage to cut short my dreams by deliberately falling.

Still asleep, I go over this dream in my mind and I repeat certain parts of it, varying the details. More specifically, this second version features a rectangle of white paper that is given to those who are about to be shot to death. They are allowed to write their last words on it, and when the time comes for them to be executed, the piece of paper is placed not over their eyes but over their mouth, like a gag.

May 20, 1944

(real-life)

Riding our bicycles (the primary means of transportation during the Occupation), Z . . . and I make our way back from a dinner at the house of friends who live in the sixteenth. Shortly before midnight (curfew hour), we reach the door of our home at 53 bis quai des Grands-Augustins and encounter a guy in a cap, around thirty to thirty-five years old, who claims he's from up North and asks us in the most friendly of fashions if we know the way to "the lost city," "the audacious city." He is probably drunk or not quite right in the head, or perhaps both? We reply that we are sorry but cannot give him directions, and he lets the matter drop.

Z . . . thinks—no doubt correctly—that he is someone who works on the river barges that are tied up on the quay directly below our house. As for me, elaborating on the theme of this river that we live next to and whose course we had just been following on our way back home, I think to myself that it might well be the city of Dis that our sooty interlocutor was seeking on the left bank of the Seine.

During that period, despite its motto (*Fluctuat nec mergitur*), Paris was also a sunken city. I realize this only now.

May 22-23, 1946

(after the grand opening of the "Madagascar" exhibit at the Musée de l'Homme)

Dr. Paul Rivet, my boss in real life (who, upon his return from America at the end of the war, has taken over the reins of the institution where I work), owns a large traveling circus somewhat like the outfit that used to be run by Colonel Cody, alias "Buffalo Bill." I make my way along a road with several friends, aware that this road will cut through the grounds that make up the immense ring of the circus. Just at this moment, a Cowboy-and-Indian show is taking place, a rodeo of sorts. Having always hated gunfire, I hope that our crossing of the circus ring will not coincide with the moment they start shooting off their pistols, a standard event in this type of show.

We arrive at the circus, but we are no longer anonymous passers-by but members of Rivet's troupe. Forming part of what in circus parlance is called the "rail," we are lined up at the entrance of the ring and are also supposed to contribute to the performance. For my part, I know that I will be a rodeo rider: I will not be expected to do tricks on horseback (all my life I've been a woefully clumsy rider); instead, I am merely to sit in the saddle, nothing more. I take off the raincoat I am wearing because it's hardly appropriate for the occasion: after all, aren't the people on the "rail" usually supposed to wear livery?

March 4-5, 1947

I am battling a winged bull on the Place du Trocadéro, in front of the entrance to the Musée de l'Homme,
but as I move in for the kill I realize it is no more
substantial than an inflatable toy. Upon waking, this
adventure leaves me with the optimistic conviction that
we tend to make too many mountains out of molehills.

In another dream (which preceded this one by some
14 years and which was in turn a later version of an
earlier dream), I was supposed to fight a boxing match
for the benefit of the Museum. I was not at all happy
with this set-up and at the very last minute I chickened
out, unabashedly declaring that I had no intention of
being punched around.

The idea that fighting should be linked to my
profession as an ethnographer no doubt has to do with
the fact that in 1931 the world bantamweight cham-
pion, Al Brown (a Panamanian black who was so
elegant in the ring that the working-class fight crowds
used to tauntingly call him "twinkle toes"), fought a
benefit match in the Cirque d'Hiver to raise money for

the Dakar-Djibouti Expedition. There is also my memory of the admission a professional boxer once made to Picasso, and which Picasso reported to me as very revealing of just how a boxer feels when he climbs into the ring: "It's as if you were going down to the bottom of the sea."

January, 1948

(Sidi Madani, near Blida)

Reflecting on the human problems that Algeria raises—problems that I have on several occasions brought up with several French residents who realized the gravity of the situation, condemned the mistakes that had been made, and were worried about the probable evolution of relations between the Moslem and non-Moslem portions of the population—I so strongly sense a showdown is inevitable that, filled with anxiety, I let out a scream.

Upon awakening, I try to remember the concrete basis for the general mood of this nightmare. A Roman tile or shiny, slippery slate shingle (a tangible object, not the ideal term of a metaphor)—this is the precise form in which the "Moslem question" appears to me.

No doubt they were far less neurotic than I, these soldiers that I had seen bursting into the marketplace

144

of Medea one morning, executing maneuvers as their commander barked out orders, forcing the worried merchants to beat a quick retreat with the meager goods they had brought from the countryside in straw baskets.

December, 1948

A realization that comes too late to make up for the omission: after I have left Antigua (in the British West Indies), it occurs to me that in visiting the island (fairly carefully at that), I completely forgot the fortified castle that is its major attraction. I deeply regret this because of all the Antilles there was perhaps no other island that seduced me to this extent.

A stopover on my way from Guadaloupe to Haiti and back, Antigua furnished me with the material for two dreams. The second dream was so sparse (or so fleeting) that it was only a few days later that I realized it had followed an earlier dream. But this recurrence could in itself be of significance.

A cascade of real and invented images; as I sort through the successive layers of memory, I reach what represents their original stage. While in Antigua I had been staying in the town of Saint John in a kind of family rooming house called the Kensington Hotel; only the blackness of the chambermaids in their little bonnets and aprons distinguished the place from

146

Great Britain. One day I traveled by car to the baths of Fort Saint James with two companions I had met on the old tub that had taken us to the island: a Dutch chemical engineer and a Frenchman who was involved in sugar manufacturing at the Marquisat Factory. Disdaining the fort (or greeting it with the briefest of glimpses), we had drunk some beer in a building perched on an elevation that was fairly cool for the late afternoon. What I liked above all about Antigua was the way its half-tropical, half-provincial atmosphere managed to achieve the heights of exotic incandescence through the double piquancy provided by England and the Empire. A sugar cane field on the flank of a small hill, a small factory with a chimney sticking into the sky, a pasture with cows and sheep, a public garden with a monument, an ancient, ever so British cemetery, cabins lining the beach as ramshackle as those on the French islands, several Portuguese or Syro-Lebanese shops, a line of mountains said to represent (according to local tradition) a Carib king lying on his back with his arms folded on his chest (and which I first caught sight of from the bay as I was coming into port)—these are the meager elements of the landscape that I manage to gather to mind, with the help of my travel diary.

This fort that I might have glimpsed but that at any rate I did not visit and whose image (more or less invented) tormented me by its very absence, this fort finds its African replica three years earlier in the fortress of Elmina in Ghana (formerly the Gold Coast). Passing through the beautiful old colonial town of Cape Coast on the route from Accra to Takoradi, I visited this fort built by the Dutch during the slave trade era to defend the trading post baptized "La Mine" by the old colonists from Dieppe but subsequently renamed "El Mina" by the Portuguese. In one of the courtyards of this barracks that is over three centuries old, I observed two British officers playing deck tennis in their swim suits. Little by little, Cape Coast and Elmina blended together in my mind into a single Elsenor planted in the midst of the tropics by Europeans more concerned about protecting their commercial interests than about conversing with ghosts. Further traces of these particular cities or of other places in this region that I inevitably think back to with nostalgia: the flashy merchandise of Hindu bazaars and the medley of colors of the cotton clothing.

Finally, the ultimate stage in this cascade of images is reached with a fortified dream castle, devoid of any military features but also situated on an island. Its image, having become so quintessential as to be barely visible, has nonetheless remained with me as one of the most blissful images ever presented to me by the phantasmagoria of sleep.

Some of my close friends and I set off on an excursion toward a rocky island off the coast of Brittany (which is in fact where we were then staying). We get to an island and are convinced we have reached our destination, but we soon realize we have made a mistake: the island we were aiming for is much further offshore and can only be reached by a rather long journey by boat. We had been the victims of an optical illusion: seen from the shore, the two islands are easily confused. Although we decide not to push on to the island we had initially aimed for, it appears to me as follows: rising out of the sea as abruptly as a citadel, it features a palace in the classical style of Versailles whose pediment is ornamented with some sort of large gilded coat of arms; below the pediment (logically: on the sea, between the edifice and ourselves), a large vessel with an aftercastle and a multitude of red sails heaves into view; above the pediment one can see the rocks of the island, a chaos of rounded masses as red and voluminous as the ship's sails. I tell my wife's brother-in-law—who remains incredulous—that I have never seen anything this beautiful before, even in Africa.

It was at Kerrariot, the night of August 18-19, 1933, after having taken a walk along the celebrated rocks of Ploumanac'h, that I dreamt of this Eldorado—in which gold mines and sugar cane plantations have no place.

Islands, cities of distant climes, castles or forts overlooking the sea: images of a region so distant, so separate that death cannot cast me back to it again.

July 13-14, 1952

(real-life)

It was two days ago that I left Basse-Terre in Guadeloupe on board the motorized yacht *La Belle Saintoise*. At Terre-De-Haut, the largest island in the archipelago of the Saints, I took room and board in the house of an old colored woman by the name of Mme Joyeux: Widow Joyeux.

Lying on a square bed that is so huge I can use its entire left side as a night table, I have been asleep for some time when I am awakened by the exquisite strains of dance music that is coming from some record player or radio and filters into my room from a neighboring house. A small combo that seems to me to be composed of a clarinet, a flute, and a guitar, playing beguines, mazurkas, and quadrilles in which I recognize—for no real reason, I admit—the old creole dance called the "haute taille."

During the following days in Guadeloupe, and then upon returning to Martinique before my flight to New

York and France, I would question various acquaintances about this music. But my inquiries lead nowhere: none of my Antillean friends had ever heard of this bewitching combination of instruments, and the riddle of this dream music would remain such an enigma that I would wonder if it had not in fact come to me in a dream.

Late 1954

(early morning, after waking up prematurely)

In need of money, I hire myself out as a bull in a corrida. As the papers are being signed, the impresario insists that I undergo an inspection to make sure that I indeed have the five horns stipulated by the contract; he has after all guaranteed that he will furnish a "bull with five horns." Two of these horns are supposedly on my head; two more are the protrusions of my shoulder blades which the impresario verifies by touching them. My wife is present and I tell her it gives me the chills to be touched there, just below my nape, on the very spot where the death-blow will fall. She says to me: "It's just a lousy morning you'll have to get through. Once it's all over, you'll feel fine . . ." I get incensed: "Once it's all over, I'll be dead!" Beside myself with rage, I shout at both of them: "You don't give a shit about me! I'm not going to fall for this!" And I add: "I'd rather take my chances as a bullfighter!'' The contract will not be signed and the dream ends there.

Almost everybody to whom I have recounted this dream has asked me where my fifth horn was located.

October 31, 1955

(between Krasnoyarsk and Novo-Sibirsk)

On a Paris street I meet two young women, both of whom are charming and attractive, even though their Salvation Army act makes them somewhat ridiculous. They are hawking a Protestant newspaper, and are trying to win me over to their cause: "What do you read? Are you politically committed?" Such are the kinds of question they ask as they try to provoke me into some real soul-searching.

I had this dream while returning from Peking as I was sleeping in the plane between two stopovers in Siberia. Both on the flight to China and back I was overwhelmed by the variety of vistas in the daylight below (above all, I remember the forests of birch and larch and maple and the steep mountains, their escarpments striated in black and white like Chinese landscape painting); and in the blackness of night I was struck by the great expanses of snow, now and then punctuated by a cluster of lights indicating some industrial center. The flight was broken up, like a stage-coach journey, into a number of stops: a layover here for a meal in a real country inn, its tables cluttered with crystalware; a layover there to spend the night in a hotel so overcrowded with passengers that it turns into a caravansary. Both on the flight out and back, my friends and I were attended to by stewardesses wearing peasant scarves on their heads or fur hats that were half-Cossack, half-Coldstream Guard, tall and jutting down over the forehead.

Upon waking, I realize that the dream I just had took place in France, whereas during my several weeks in China all my dreams were Chinese (though my dreams were rare because my busy schedule left few hours for any sleep with the density of dream). In this particular dream—the only one I had the time to note down during my visit to the Far East—is there any local color I can find? None whatsoever, unless it has to do (perhaps) with the kindness of these two women and their cheerful commitment to their cause. Among our interpreters and among the various people we met in Peking and elsewhere, there were a number of these girls or women whose earnestness only added to their attractiveness; as certain women inspire dreams of pleasure, so these women made me dream of political activism and commitment.

At Krasnoyarsk, I set my watch to local time and noted that we had landed at 8:25 P.M. and not at 1:25 P.M. as my watch indicated. We landed at Novo-Sibirsk at 11:40 P.M. (according to my watch which I had reset when we changed time-zones). But in the cafeteria where we are waiting to reboard our flight, the clock says 3:45 A.M., so I can't figure out what the hell is going on . . .

155

August 9-10,1957

The setting (probably) is the distant regions of Asia. The sun is shining brightly and I am standing on a terrace or some other elevated spot situated ten or so meters above an outdoor swimming pool. The pool is huge and differs from what in my dream I term an "olympic swimming pool" (that is, geometrical in form like most swimming pools) as much as a Chinese garden, for example, differs from a French garden designed in the well-groomed style of Le Nôtre.

Instead of being a rectangular pool well-defined by cement edges and featuring a diving board whose metal framework is painted white (to protect against rust and to add a decorative touch), this particular pool is an irregularly shaped pond whose banks slope down slightly and whose elegant curves I admire. Here and there at the bottom of the translucid pool I see bunches of bushy vegetation, particularly ferns—which, although not as high as fern trees, are nonetheless far superior in size to the ferns of our climate. On the sandy bottom of the pool, as if they had no problem breathing, are a number of lovely little yellow-skinned boys and girls who, virtually naked, are playing or resting among the ferns and, no doubt, the fish.

I realize that these children are far from being exceptional athletes and that, having become accustomed to subaquatic life, it is entirely natural for them to spend unlimited periods of time under water. Their grace and their placidity, the bister-colored sand and yellow hue of their skin, the curvilinear design of the pool, the green of the large ferns that almost graze the surface of the water that is unruffled by any breeze and undisturbed by any breaking bubble, the fine hot weather—all this blends together in a very happy fashion and the joy I feel in contemplating this scene is as peaceful as it is profound.

A slight shadow seems to fall across the scene, however, when I realize that I would have just as much difficulty swimming in this enchanting pool as in any other because my feet would no doubt get entangled in the luxuriant vegetation.

September 1957

(real-life, Florence)

On the Piazza del Duomo, in front of the gaudy conglomeration formed by the cathedral, the campanile, and the baptistery (large coffee cream cakes composed of alternating strata of white and dark green filling), several dromedaries and a camel pass by, led by a black cavalier wearing a large, flowing white cloak that is Arab or Sudanese in style.

Having pitched its tents on the Campo di Marte, the Togni Circus was putting on its parade that morning: the caravan of the Magi, such as one sees in old canvasses where the painter has selected the monuments of his own city to provide an anachronistic decor.

September 29-30, 1957

(Florence)

Z . . . and I have stopped for tea in a very fine-looking home that is either a private residence or a deluxe rooming house (such as the one we actually visited a few days ago on the outskirts of Florence and whose owner was an English woman whose studied elegance was a bit annoying). The servants prepare tea for us. They bump into each other, jostle for position, squabble, drop or tip over objects: a real knockabout farce out of *commedia dell'arte*. At least one of these servants, sporting a striped apron, is obviously drunk. We are seated on a low couch, I on the right and Z . . . on the left. The drunken servant is standing directly next to me, trying to catch the china (plates? platters?) that has been piled on a nearby piece of furniture. The china crashes to the floor, almost hitting Z . . . on the head. Which is why I suggest we trade places.

Tea is finally served. A servant wearing a white barman's vest passes around a large platter filled with

159

thick, circular pastry containing jam in the middle. As etiquette requires, I take the nearest piece—it turns out to be the smallest one, which is just as well because I am not really hungry. I bite into the pastry and the jam oozes out onto my chin. The servant rushes to my assistance and places the platter (as if it were a shaving mug) directly under my chin so that the jam won't ruin my clothes if it drips off the bottom of my face. Then, with his fingers, he stuffs the remainder of the pastry into my mouth. This is the straw that breaks the camel's back. Beside myself with anger, I get up, take a few steps toward the center of the room, and shout: "Where the hell are we anyway?" Then I launch into a lengthy protest against the force-feeding to which I have been submitted: do they think I am some animal? What is this, some kind of zoo?

Soon my *where are we anyway?* takes on a Hamletic turn. I repeat my question in a distraught fashion as if, prey to some metaphysical vertigo, I had gone mad. It is then that I notice in the corner of the room a steep stone stairway leading downward. Fairly narrow, it is lit by windows (or skylights) with stained glass. I am about to hurl myself headfirst down this stairway and smash my skull on the landing just to be done with it once and for all when Z . . . (roused from her real sleep by the screams I am beginning to emit) calls out to me and wakes me.

January 6, 1958

(real-life, Neuilly-sur-Seine)

After having been anesthetized for minor surgery, I find myself back in my hospital bed. At first, it seems to me that I have been in this bed all the while, but this erroneous impression is soon put right, and I try to recap everything that has happened. I am seized by great anxiety because I can locate no slice of lapsed time, however abstract, corresponding to the density of time that has passed, without my knowledge, between the sudden plunge I took after the pentothal injection and the moment I reawoke in my hospital room. No sleep is quite like this sort of blank or void. Whereas with sleep one can always more or less measure its opacity or duration, here was something that seemed never to have existed at all: at one fell swoop, you sink into something undescribable, and then you are back on your feet again.

Like some strange lesion, this experience would continue to haunt me for some time—it was not so much the void that bothered me, but rather the gaping fault-line represented by this truly *dead time* that had been cut out of my life by the stroke of an axe.

May 18-19, 1958

I am a tourist in some city which, upon waking, I am unable to identify as French or to connect to any of the particular countries I am familiar with. I am there in the company of several close acquaintances whose identities also remain uncertain, although my wife was along (this I am fairly sure of) and perhaps also those three friends with whom—it was several days ago, just prior to the sedition in France that brought about the collapse of the Fourth Republic— we were wandering around the zoo in Basel and came across a white peacock who, in order to seduce his hen,, was spreading out his tail and rustling his feathers in front of her like a ship's rigging vibrating under the pressure of a purely internal breeze, almost impercep- tibly fluttering his openwork fan like some samurai or roué, and occasionally sketching out a slow giratory movement as if he were trying to take better advantage of the wind or attempting to present his mesmerizing screen at a more efficient angle. An unknown and probably foreign city, very likely one of those cities

163

Artemidoros of Ephesus claims it is unlucky to see in a dream.

Someone informed us—or perhaps we read it somewhere—that near the center of the city there was an establishment devoted to the art of divination. The place is apparently not too hard to locate, seeing as how it occupies an entire building whose exterior (as we know) resembles those nightclubs that exist in the redlight districts of every country in the world or else those establishments, more discreet but equally recognizable, that are commonly called "houses of illusion." Nonetheless we still don't have the faintest idea as to the precise appearance of the place; the only information we have is negative: its exterior differs considerably from that of other buildings.

We wander around this way and that—the complete loss of direction no doubt reflects (from what I can remember of it) the disoriented gait of so many of our dreams. Finally we arrive at a street that is fairly narrow and that has no sidewalks, similar to the ancient streets of so many Mediterranean cities (even though I mention this slight hint of locale, there is in fact nothing precise that would incline this fragment of urban decor more to the south than to the north or more to a sunny than to a cloudy clime). There we see a building whose oddity strikes us immediately: its facade is far taller than normal, given the narrowness of the building, and it is covered with anthropo- and zoomorphic statues, or at least with moldings whose gothic or baroque style brings to mind either those decorations one sees on town halls in German or Flemish countries, or else the opulent ornamentation of an 18th-century synagogue or of a Catholic edifice which I can in retrospect get a fairly good idea of by evoking an abandoned church in Venice in front of which I used to occasionally pass, a church transformed into a movie house and located in the old commercial quarter of the Mazarie, not far from the small square where the bronze statue of Goldoni, cane in hand and three-cornered hat on his head, appears to be just another figure among the strollers or passers-by, even though it is situated somewhat higher in space and at a certain distance in time. A figure whose sudden appearance in a dream could only be comforting: a faded glory now transformed into this little friendly fellow with a cheery face and a spring in his step.

Convinced that this profusely decorated building is indeed the one we are eager to visit, we enter. But here again I can remember nothing precise—i.e. calling out to the supposed residents of the place, knocking at the door, or ringing the doorbell—that would allow me to go beyond the abstract quality of this "we enter," which is just as vague as the group of acquaintances accompanying me, the geographical location of the city, and the actual style of the facade—despite my somewhat arbitrary evocation of Venitian memory in an attempt to reconstruct the impression it made upon me.

Whoever it was that ushered us in or however it was that we got there, once inside the place we find ourselves in an interior that is rather dark (somewhat like those antique stores where the objects on display are perfectly visible but where the light seems completely absorbed by the clutter) and then realize we are in the presence of a woman whom we immediately recognize as the lady of the house, in other words, as the prophetess. She is seated several meters from the threshold, most likely on a simple chair, her back three quarters turned. She is an old black woman—or

165

Ethiopian—who is quite shriveled and she is wearing her hair in a dirty white veil. Her image (not immediately but as I later try to recompose it) reminds me of those many matrons I encountered in Africa or Haiti who rule over spiritistic cults and who make a profit from medical treatments, from predictions, from magical operations that they insist are legitimate and not sorcery, laying down the law, sometimes actually wearing pants, using their authority to sort out conflicting interests, and occasionally intervening in marriages or divorces with all the respect that is due to them because of the privileged relationship they are believed to have with those supernatural powers who, under the eyes of the faithful, cause them to theatrically flutter or gesticulate about in a state of trance.

Standing slightly to the rear toward the right edge of the mantelpiece is another dark-skinned woman, but she is younger, taller, and more robust. She is wearing a long, loose African tunic made out of dark cotton fabric. This beautiful, regal creature is no doubt a disciple who functions as a servant to the older woman whose superior talents have subjugated her.

At the outset we see a spacious hall that somewhat resembles a public or reserve reading room in a municipal or national library. Innumerable volumes, obviously very old to judge from their rich, faded bindings, are arranged in bookcases whose shelves and uprights are made of gray metal. The bookcase we can see best—half-way down the hall and running from one side of it to the other—contains a thick iron sword about ten meters long and surely very heavy that is lying horizontally on the books, some of which are standing, some of which are lying, some of which are open, some of which are closed, and all of which appear not to have been consulted for months or years

166

but merely seem to be displayed there like stage props. In other bookcases we cannot see, there are other swords crushing other volumes, swords identical in size and make, with the same old-fashioned hilt. This signifies (and I am aware of this even in the dream) that *one takes no account of books here.* The prophecies are made not on any scientific basis but entirely by visionary means, and it is the seances devoted to supernatural possession that constitute the most obvious activity of the place. Among the books stored in the large ground-floor hall (the only portion of the establishment that we visited, for the dream ends there, as if the gigantic sword we saw had cut short the possibility of any continuation), there are a number of works on magic, but like the totality of printed knowledge (however irrational it might be), they too are nullified by the weight of this sword.

July 14-15, 1958

"Poulet Vulliambert (or Vuilliambeau, or Vulli-
ambé)"—the first and last names of a hooker or bar
girl who gave me her telephone number in a aaaa-
nightclub where we had struck up a conversation.
Someone (maybe me) has clumsily taken his finger-
nail and ripped the slip of paper or cardboard on
which I had noted down the number. How recover it,
unless it be by going to sleep again and making my
way back to this woman whom I had so enjoyed
chatting with for several hours?

I fall back asleep, but to no avail: my little escapade
is over and done with. If I renarrate it in writing, is
this not merely another tactic to recapture some small
portion of this adventure and, if chance permits, to
breathe in its perfume once again?

November 6-7, 1960

"Charity! Charity!" I am wandering through the streets of an unfamiliar neighborhood, trying to catch a small dog who bears the name of this theological virtue. He was given to me by a baker; I was careless enough to walk him without a leash, and he ran away. A butcher (or some other shopkeeper) has already had a good laugh hearing me call after the dog that he has just watched race by. Shouting at the top of my lungs like some incensed beggar, I could very well be taken for a village idiot or for an escaped lunatic whom the police will swiftly move to arrest. Who cares. I go on shouting as loudly as I can, not only because I am so mortified at the loss of the little dog but also because I am drunk with the sound of my own voice: "Charity! Charity!"

The Eridanos Library

Eridanos Press, Inc., P.O. Box 211, Hygiene, CO 80533.

*This book was printed in March of 1988 by
Il Poligrafico Piemontese P.P.M. in Casale Monferrato, Italy.
The Type is Baskerville 12/13.
The paper is Corolla Book 120 grs. for the insides
and Acquerello Bianco 160 grs. for the jacket,
both manufactured by Cartiera Fedrigoni, Verona,
especially for this collection.*